Hero of the Yacolt Burn

Hero of the Yacolt Burn

Douglas N. Maynard

RESOURCE *Publications* · Eugene, Oregon

Resource Publications
An Imprint of Wipf and Stock Publishers
199 W. 8th Ave., Suite 3
Eugene, OR 97401

www.wipfandstock.com

PAPERBACK ISBN: 978-1-6667-3714-1
HARDCOVER ISBN: 978-1-6667-9626-1
EBOOK ISBN: 978-1-6667-9627-8

JUNE 14, 2022 11:47 AM

To my wife, for all the love and commitment to our marriage over the past thirty-five years. I love you!

Contents

Preface

As a child, I often stood looking out my grandparents' large picture windows at the hills and wondered why so many of the trees looked like they were charred. I was told it was because of the Yacolt Burn. Years later, in high school, I learned more about the burn, but it wasn't until I became a Pacific Northwest history teacher myself and delved much deeper into the origins of the fire that I understood just how much it had impacted the Lewis River Valley in which I had grown up.

Prologue

Connecting the Dots

ONE OF THE MOST interesting things I enjoy about history is the ability to look back and connect the dots. The past, present, and future are all connected, but it is only when we step back and look at them in retrospect that we can understand their connections.

The Oregon Country encompassed the present-day states of Oregon, Washington, and Idaho and the Canadian province of British Columbia.

The first Europeans to explore the area were the Spanish. From their New World headquarters in Mexico, a number of Spanish explorers sailed the waters along the West Coast of the United States and Canada between 1542 and 1819. They recorded the existence of a major river they called the San Rogue River, which would later be changed to the Columbia River. They explored what they named the Strait of Juan de Fuca and the islands of the north Puget Sound. But the Spanish had a single-minded purpose, finding gold; and having determined through their interaction with the native people of the area that there was none, they abandoned any further exploration.

The Spanish were followed by the British, who came to the area not to plunder but to find a water passage across the North American continent to the Pacific Ocean. They chose to explore the Pacific Northwest coast to find this passage because the Spanish had written about a river flowing east to west. But the mouth of this Pacific Northwest river was elusive, and in time, it took on an almost mythical presence.

While the British found neither the Northwest Passage nor the mouth of the Columbia River, they did find valuable resources—not gold or silver but fish, furs, and timber. Of the three, the most lucrative would be the fur trade, and the most desired fur was the beaver pelt.

The discovery of the mouth of the Columbia River would fall to the American Robert Gray.

While the U.S., Britain, and even Russia competed for control of the fur trade in the Pacific Northwest, the ultimate winner was Britain and its surrogate, the Hudson Bay Company. Although economic control of the area appeared squarely in the hands of the British, the geographic ownership of the Oregon Territory was clearly in dispute.

While the number of citizens occupying the area favored the British, the most important time-honored tradition of international land claims belonged to the United States, because of Robert Gray's discovery. The tradition was that the first country to record the discovery of a previously unclaimed river system could claim all lands drained by the river system, including all of the river's tributaries. An undisputed claim would have included both the discovery of the river's source and the river's mouth. The United States owned the right of the discovery for the Columbia River's mouth, but the Columbia's source as of yet had not been discovered.

Enter Thomas Jefferson, the Louisiana Purchase, and Lewis and Clark. When the chance to purchase from France the vast territory west of the Mississippi River known as Louisiana presented itself in 1803, President Jefferson quickly seized the opportunity. The ink on the agreement was barely dry when President Jefferson launched an expedition led by Lewis and Clark. The expedition was charged with numerous tasks, one of which was to determine the source of the Columbia River. President Jefferson was clearly thinking about solidifying the United States's claim to the Oregon Country.

The results of the Lewis and Clark expedition were many, but only one is relevant to the beginning of this story: there were vast amounts of Native Americans living in the Oregon region who were un-Christianized.

That revelation sparked many Christian organizations to recruit missionaries to send to the wilderness to save the souls of these un-Christianized Native Americans.

The success of these missionaries who came to Oregon to convert the Native Americans to Christianity was minimal at best. These same missionaries had a much greater impact on influencing U.S. citizens to migrate to Oregon.

Two of the most outspoken missionaries about the virtues of Oregon were Marcus Whitman and Jason Lee. Upon arriving in Oregon, it soon became clear to Lee that, while ministering to the Native Americans was a worthwhile endeavor, their conversion would be a more daunting task. He soon changed his focus to meeting the needs of the few white settlers in the area and promoting greater settlement by American citizens.

Manifest destiny was the belief it was "God's will" that the United States should stretch from the Atlantic Ocean to the Pacific Ocean. Several people are credited with first using the term. One such person was John O' Sullivan, newspaper editor from New York City, who used his editorials to push for the annexation of the Oregon Country. Also credited with first using the term is missionary Jason Lee. While O' Sullivan espoused it in his newspaper column, Lee preached it from the pulpit. He had come to the conclusion that God had brought him to Oregon for the purpose of insuring Oregon would become part of the United States. His motto became "Oregon, for God and Country." In 1838, Jason Lee embarked on a preaching tour across America, espousing the positive attributes of Oregon, and calling on Christians to fulfill God's will by moving to Oregon.

In 1839, a group of men who had heard Lee's message embarked for Oregon. Known as the Peoria Party, they were the first true U.S. emigrants to travel the Oregon Trail for the purpose of helping the U. S. claim Oregon.

Thomas Merriman, at age sixteen, attended one of Jason Lee's messages about the Oregon Country and was convinced he should migrate to Oregon. At age eighteen, he began this journey.

From exploration by the Spanish, to manifest destiny, to Thomas Merriman, the dots have been connected. We can now proceed to our story of Thomas Merriman:

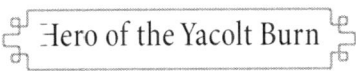

Hero of the Yacolt Burn

Introduction

My name is Tyler N. Elliot. I am the great-grandson of T. Y. Elliot, not T. S. Eliot, the great British poet. Tyler Yonder Elliot, known to most as Yonder, was a far less famous newspaper reporter (although he did have his moment of fame) who worked for the *Oregon Journal* in Portland, Oregon, from 1902 to 1942.

Let's start where I came into this story. About a year ago, I inherited the home of my grandmother. As I was cleaning the place and throwing out the trash, I uncovered a tin box full of papers. I began thumbing through the documents. There were a dozen or so stock certificates, and my first thought was, I've hit the jackpot, I'm going to be rich!

I took the tin home and carefully began going through the papers. It turns out the stocks were all worthless, but there were several very carefully folded, fragile newspaper articles, aged by years of time, and a dog-eared manuscript.

As I carefully unfolded the newspaper articles, I was amazed; they were all the same story, "Hero of the Yacolt Burn," but the newspapers were different. There was a copy from *The Globe* from New York City and one from the *Chicago Tribune*, as well as copies from the *San Francisco Call* and the *Fort Wayne Weekly Sentinel*. The byline on each of the stories was T. Y. Elliot.

As I read the original and a follow-up story published in the *Oregon Journal*, it was clear Great-Grandfather was enthralled with the subject of his newspaper articles. When I opened the manuscript and began to read, I understood why. The manuscript style is of a newspaper man interviewing his subject. I hope you will enjoy it as much I have.

The first thing a reporter is taught is there are four significant elements to every story: who, what, where, and how. But the naked facts don't make a story good; they only set the stage for the character or characters of the story to draw the reader in and give the story a heart. Great stories, on the other hand, have more than a heart; they have a soul that transcends time.

What follows is the previously unpublished manuscript "Hero of the Yacolt Burn."

> I have added additional information in text boxes to help supplement the historical perspective when it's useful.

I forgot to mention, like Great-Grandpa, I'm a writer myself.

The Unpublished Manuscript of T. Y. Elliot

IF A MAN IS the sum of all his experiences, Thomas Merriman is a man whose sum far exceeds most others. I first met Thomas in 1902 while covering the natural disaster known as the Yacolt Burn. The fire broke out in mid-September and consumed thousands of acres of land and claimed thirty-eight lives. If not for Mr. Merriman, the death toll would have been much higher.

In the wake of the fire's devastation, I reported how, after moving his family to a small sandbar in the middle of the Lewis River, he sent his two sons on horseback, one west, the other north, to warn neighbors. Thomas, with a wagon drawn by a team of horses, headed east, into the smoke and fast-approaching blaze to help fellow community residents. Three hours after leaving his family, he returned, leading five other wagons carrying six families, totaling twenty-seven lives. The small sandbar, now crowded, held more than one hundred souls, as they awaited the impending danger to arrive. As the fire reached their location, burning embers began falling from the sky, and heavy smoke descended upon them, filling their lungs and stinging their eyes. As the fire lapped at the river's edges, the inhabitants left the small sandbar and took refuge in the frigid water of the river, to emerge an hour or more later, after the fire had passed them by.

> September 11–13, 1902, saw the largest fire in Washington State history sweep through Yacolt, Washington. The fire is now infamously known as the Yacolt Burn. The fire's origin is still unknown; however, there was speculation at the time that it was an accident resulting from local loggers working. The fire burned over 370 square miles and resulted in thirty-eight fatalities in the Lewis River area.

As the survivors emerged from the banks of the river, they saw an intermittent pattern of destruction. There were patches of green grass surrounded by blackened earth. Trees still burning, while others stood untouched. Mr. Merriman's home and outbuildings had suffered no major damage, but one of his sons' homes was completely destroyed. Of the families the Merrimans helped rescue, all survived, but most had suffered the loss of a structure and/or animals.

You might think what Mr. Merriman did was courageous but maybe not extraordinary. I forgot to mention Mr. Merriman was seventy-nine years old at the time.

After the first story about Mr. Merriman and the Yacolt Burn was so successful, I decided to write a follow-up piece a year later. It was during this period that we became great friends, and I asked if I could write about his life. To which he agreed.

CHAPTER 1

∞∞

First Interview: Early Experiences

ONE THING I LEARNED early on as a writer: when conducting an interview, say as little as possible, and listen intently.

Thomas, I asked others to describe you, and they used words like: loyal, hard worker, dreamer, a great storyteller, a true friend, music lover, wise, risk-taker, thoughtful, well-read, and God-fearing!

I asked your son what he thought has made you the man you are today, and he said, "More than anything else, his early life experiences!"

Can you tell me about a few of these experiences?

In 1828, my family, and my father's brother and his wife Sara, decided to leave Western Virginia and move their families to Missouri.

They purchased a tract of land, traveling by horse and wagon about an hour east of Independence, Missouri. They quickly went about clearing two home sites, building log cabins, and setting up a sawmill. The land was covered with a large variety of oak, elm, red cedar, and white pine trees.

The large parcel had a swift meandering creek that came from further up in the mountains. They built a waterwheel, then dammed the creek and diverted a portion of the water to power the sawmill. During the summer, they cut trees and hauled or floated them to the mill; in the winter, they cut the logs into slabs and dimensional lumber. During the fall and spring, they used a team of horses and a wagon to deliver their products to willing buyers.

I was five years old at the time, but I remember the move well. More importantly, I remember my Father's determination to make a better life for his family.

I sometimes rode along with my father on his delivery trips to Independence, and we'd talk. He'd tell me stories from the Bible, and I'd listen intently. He always said, there are five important things to having a good life. If you always work hard and are honest, people will respect you; the closest thing to heaven you will experience here on earth is the love of your family, so love your wife like she's the most precious thing on this earth and raise your children to be God-fearing, and they will be a joy and not a burden. Be resolute and never be afraid to dream; but, above all, love God with all your heart.

When we moved to Missouri, we were a family of four, my parents, my little brother Daniel, and I. Although, within a few years, we were a family of seven, as my sisters Kathleen, Victoria, and Mary were born in successive years. Mother kept the house, milked the cows, and took care of the garden; I fed and watered the horses and cows; Daniel cared for the chickens. Father and Uncle Dan worked from sunup to nearly sundown six days a week at the sawmill or at logging. Even though Father worked long hours, he always found at least a small amount of time to spend with us. Sometimes we'd throw horseshoes, other times we'd play checkers, but I always looked forward to the Bible stories he would tell before bedtime. He could tell a story like no one else I knew. My favorite was David and Goliath. When he started talking, I would close my eyes, and I could see the characters come to life.

The Philistines were the enemies of Israel and were about to attack them. Saul, king of the Israelites, was aware of their impending attack, and had assembled his army to fight. The Philistines occupied one hill and the Israelites another.

A man named Goliath was in the Philistine camp. He was nearly ten feet tall. He wore a bronze helmet on his head and a coat of armor. As weapons, he carried a bronze javelin, a spear, and a shield.

Goliath stood and shouted to the ranks of Israel, "Choose a man and have him come down to me. If he is able to fight and kill me, we will become your subjects; but if I overcome him and kill him, you will become our subjects and serve us."

For forty days, Goliath came forward every morning and evening to make his challenge.

David had three brothers in the army of Israel. Because he was the youngest and just a boy, he was left at home to help his father, who was very old, and to tend to the family's animals. One day, David's father instructed him to take food and supplies to his brothers fighting against the Philistines.

When David arrived, he witnessed Goliath's daily challenge and his cursing against the God of Israel. David asked, "Who is this Philistine that he should defy the armies of the living God? And why has no one accepted his challenge?"

The soldiers told him his name is Goliath, and everyone here is afraid; the stories of how many he had already killed were rampant. They said, "King Saul will give great wealth to the man who kills him. He will also give him his daughter in marriage."

David said, "I will fight him."

What David said was overheard and reported to King Saul, and Saul sent for him.

David said to Saul, "Let no one lose heart on account of this Philistine; your servant will go and fight him."

Saul replied, "You are only a boy, and he has been a warrior from his youth. How can you hope to defeat him?"

David said to Saul, "When a lion or a bear came and carried off a sheep from my flock, I went after it, struck it, and rescued the sheep from its mouth. When it turned on me, I seized it by its hair, struck it, and killed it. Your servant has killed both the lion and the bear; this Philistine will be like one of them, because he has defied the armies of the living God. The Lord who rescued me from the paw of the lion and the bear will rescue me from the hand of this Philistine."

Saul said to David, "Go, and the Lord be with you."

Then Saul put a coat of armor on David and a bronze helmet on his head. David fastened on his sword and tried walking around, but because he was not used to them, it didn't feel right.

"I cannot go in these," he said to Saul. So, he took them off. Then he took his staff in his hand, chose five smooth stones from the stream, put them in the pouch of his shepherd's bag, and with his sling in his hand, went out to meet Goliath.

When Goliath looked at David and saw that he was little more than a boy, glowing with health and handsome, he despised him. He said to David, "Am I a dog that you come at me with sticks?" And the Philistine cursed David by his gods. "Come here," he said, "and I'll give your flesh to the birds and the wild animals!"

David said to Goliath, "You come against me with sword and spear and javelin, but I come against you in the name of the Lord Almighty, the God of the armies of Israel, whom you have defied. This day, the Lord will deliver you into my hands, and I'll strike you down and cut off your head. This very day, I will give the carcasses of the Philistine army to the birds and the wild animals, and the whole world will know there is a God in Israel, and it is not by sword or spear the Lord saves; for the battle is the Lord's, and he will give all of you into our hands."

As Goliath moved closer to attack, David ran quickly toward the battle line to meet him. Reaching into his bag and taking out a stone, he slung it and struck Goliath on the forehead. The stone sank into his forehead, and he fell face down on the ground.

David ran and stood over him. He took hold of the Philistine's sword and drew it from the sheath. After he killed him, he cut off his head with the sword.

When the Philistines saw that their hero was dead, they turned and ran. The men of Israel shouted and pursued the Philistines as they retreated. Their dead were strewn along the road. When the Israelites returned from chasing the Philistines, they plundered their camp.

David took the Philistine's head and brought it to Jerusalem; he put Goliath's weapons in his own tent.

As Saul watched David going out to meet Goliath, he asked the commander of his army, "Whose son is that young man?"

The commander replied, "As surely as you live, Your Majesty, I don't know."

> *The king said, "Find out who the father of this young man is!"*
>
> *As soon as David returned from killing Goliath, he was brought to Saul, with David still holding the Philistine's head.*
>
> *"Whose son are you, young man?" Saul asked him.*
>
> *David said, "I am the son of your servant Jesse of Bethlehem."[1]*

Sunday was the Day of the Lord, and we were Methodists! It was a day of rest and play, and that included music. My father played the fiddle, my uncle the guitar, and my mother the piano. Most every Sunday, Father gave us children a lesson on his fiddle, and by the time I was eight, I could play several simple songs.

At the age of ten, I began helping my father at the mill during the summer, and Daniel took over my chores. For the first six years in Missouri, times were good, then sales began to slow down as America entered into a period of recession and then depression. As prices dropped, my father just worked harder, until the winter of 1837, when he fell ill and then suddenly died of pneumonia.

A few months later, with five mouths to feed and with no means of support, mother decided to accept the hand of another man who lived in Independence. He was willing to take in the girls but had no desire to raise Daniel or me. It was not that she didn't love Daniel and me; it was that she knew there was no other way. She was still young, attractive, and desirable, but ready-made families are a hard sell to a man who fancies a family of his own making.

Distraught but determined, Mother left us in the care of our uncle and aunt and told us to work hard to earn our keep. I was fourteen, and Daniel was twelve. Mother and Uncle Dan agreed when I came of age, my brother and I would own an equal share of the mill and my parents' property, but until then, he was to oversee and manage the mill and property the best he could. We saw mother and the girls only once or twice each month from that period forward.

Uncle Dan decided to offer Aunt Sara's brother a job if he'd move his family from Virginia to Missouri. They arrived in early spring and moved into my

---

1. 1 Sam 17.

parent's house. At first, I was angry, but I got over it. Aunt Sara's brother had a family of five, and they needed a house. Their daughter Whitney was the same age as Daniel, and their sons were nine and eight.

During the next year, the economy only got worse, but the Depression spurred many to look for greener pastures, which caused the price of lumber to pick back up, and Uncle got the business moving forward again. A few more families moved into the area, and a school was established. I had never been to school, but Mother had taught me to read from the Bible and I could print all the letters of the alphabet. Uncle Dan sent Daniel and his children to school, along with Aunt Sara's brother's children, Whitney and her brothers. Each morning, I took them to school in the wagon and returned for them in the afternoon. Whitney always sat up front with me and shared what she had learned about each day.

When I was fifteen, Uncle Dan gave me my parents' house and began paying me a weekly wage. Whitney's parents built a place of their own about a half-mile away. My mother and the girls came from Independence, we had a big party, and they stayed the weekend with us. At first, it felt odd, but Aunt Sara made sure we didn't starve to death, and Whitney visited and read books to us.

In 1838, the Reverend Jason Lee stopped at our little Methodist church to share about his work as a missionary in the Oregon Country. He was raising money to further the cause of Christianizing the Indians, as well as recruiting Methodist families to move to Oregon. He claimed it was our patriotic duty to populate Oregon. It was America's destiny to stretch from sea to sea, and we could help in this endeavor by giving money or by joining him in Oregon. "It is our duty as Americans, Christians, and Methodists to answer this calling," he said.

In 1832, four Native American men traveled to St. Louis and requested of William Clark, governor of the Louisiana Territory, for someone to bring the "Book of Heaven" to their tribes. An account of this meeting was published, and a response was received from the Methodist Church. They agreed they would send someone. Their choice to lead this mission was Jason Lee.

Jason Lee, his nephew Daniel, and three other men left New York in March of 1834, their destination Independence, Missouri. There, they joined sixty-seven other men, led by Nathaniel Wyeth. The party departed for Oregon on April 28.

Their intentions were to settle and preach to the Flatheads or one of the Salish tribes, but John McLoughlin, head of the Hudson's Bay Company's fur trading operations at Fort Vancouver, convinced the Lees a better choice would be to build a mission in the Willamette Valley.

While the valley was hospitable and well-suited for farming, it was not a great choice for a mission. The native population was dying. The spread of disease was epidemic, and each new wave brought death to thousands of the native population who had no natural immunity.

Within six years of Jason Lee's arrival, the vast majority of the Native Americans in the Willamette Valley had perished, while the number of U.S. citizens had steadily increased. The focus of the Lees' ministry was changing; it was now concentrated more on serving the new settlers of the Oregon Country and less on the Native Americans.

Lee had picked up the flag of manifest destiny and was waving it fervently. He believed God had ordained that the United States should stretch from the Atlantic to the Pacific Ocean and that the Oregon Country, which was jointly occupied by the U.S. and the British, should belong to the United States. He not only believed it, he began preaching it, giving speeches across the eastern United States, encouraging U.S. citizens to move to the Oregon Country and help claim it for America.

Rev. Lee described the Willamette Valley as a garden of Eden. The soil was so rich and productive, it could grow anything; there were sparkling clear rivers full of salmon and trees so big, it took two days to cut them down! The air was fresh and fragrant with the smell of honeysuckle and other wild flowers. Single men could claim three hundred twenty acres; married men could claim six hundred forty acres free. The Indians were pleasant people who lived off the land and had lived peacefully with the white people for over forty years.

The use of the term "Native American" refers to Indigenous People. It came into widespread use during the Civil Rights era of the 1960's and 1970's.

My head began swimming as I began thinking about trees that huge and the money I could make if I set up a sawmill. That night, Daniel and I discussed what Rev. Lee had said, and I dreamed of nothing but huge evergreen trees and sawmill blades cutting lumber.

When Whitney came over the next evening, I asked her what she thought about Oregon, and would she ever consider leaving her family, knowing she might never see them again, for the possibilities Oregon might provide a young couple.

So, you got married and headed for Oregon?

Not exactly!

I knew going to Oregon at the age of fifteen was not a possibility; neither Mother nor Uncle Dan would approve of such an idea. However, a strong, prepared eighteen-year-old would be a different story. Therefore, I began to make plans. At first, I just kept them to myself, but within a few months, I brought Daniel into them. I started saving the money Uncle was paying me, and I did a few odd jobs to earn a little extra. I especially tried to learn everything about the sawmill business. I asked my uncle to let me take on more responsibility. I learned how to file the blades, how to repair the inner working of the machinery. I took careful measurements of every board in the waterwheel. I made a list of what I thought I would need and talked to Mr. Sowers, the hardware store owner in Independence, about the cost of each item. I convinced Mr. Beck, the blacksmith in Independence, to allow me to apprentice under him, with Uncle Dan's approval.

Soon, Uncle Dan felt comfortable enough to allow me to saw logs on my own.

By age seventeen, I had decided I was going to go Oregon, and I was confident I could do it. It was time to take the final steps. Daniel was always my confidant, but I wanted to make sure his heart was set on this venture as much as mine. We discussed it, and I told him not to answer me until he had considered it very carefully. I told him, he must consider he might never see our mother or sisters ever again; there was a possibility we might die on the trip or once we got there. There was no guarantee a sawmill would be successful, and we could fail. I explained I had made up my mind, and I loved him, but this decision he had to make for himself and not out of loyalty to me.

A couple of weeks later, Daniel told me he was absolutely sure, he wanted to go.

The next step was to discuss the decision with Mother and Uncle Dan. Daniel and I traveled together to Independence the next Sunday. I broke the news to the whole family as softly as possible, and after considerable weeping by all, Mother gave us her blessing. The next big step was to tell Uncle Dan. I waited until after work on Monday to ask if I could come over to talk to him after supper. My stomach was in knots as I knocked on the door. I was clueless how he might react to my plans. So, I just blurted it out. I said, "I'm planning on leaving and going to Oregon, there are posters in Independence advertising for a wagon train to leave next spring." Then I sat and waited. He looked at me for long time and then said, "You have obviously thought about this a great deal. Tell me more."

"My plan, is I am going to go first, and Daniel will follow in two years. I will write and tell him where I have settled. Rev. Lee says a single man can claim three hundred and twenty acres in the Oregon Country, and the trees there nearly reach heaven. I plan to claim land covered with trees and set up a sawmill. New settlers in Oregon are going to need lumber!"

Once again, he looked at me for a long time and then said, "That seems rightfully so, but it's also going to be costly."

I said, "Daniel and I have been saving our money, I've talked to Mr. Sowers at the hardware store about the cost of the items I will need and I think we can swing it. I just need to have your blessing, your promise Daniel can stay, and you will start paying him like you did when I turned sixteen. He'll be sixteen in a few months, he's stronger than me, and he will work hard."

He looked at me again and said, "This is what I'd like to do, Daniel can certainly stay with us, and I will start to pay you both immediately. Since your father's death, I have thought of you both like sons. Your father and I had a dream to leave Western Virginia and come west. We slaved to clear a few acres, build two homes, and a sawmill. We worked side by side for years. He was my best friend. When I look at you, I see his spirit, his drive, the dreamer with all of the plans. I have always planned to make you and your brother partners with me, but I think God has another destination for you."

"I have already purchased a new sawmill," Uncle Dan said. "The one we have now is a little slow but has plenty of life in it still. I had planned to sell it, but now I know God was just getting it ready for you. It's yours. I have put aside some money for both you and your brother since your father's death, and I planned to give it to you once you turned eighteen; but what I think I'd rather do instead is give you your share of the money now and pay you and Daniel for your father's half-interest in the land we bought together in the two years before Daniel leaves, if we can agree on a fair price now. We paid two thousand dollars for this parcel of land thirteen years ago. I reckon it's worth twice that much now. My offer is to provide room and board to Daniel, pay him two dollars a week for working, and two thousand dollars for the property. If you agree, I will have the papers drawn up, and you and your mother can sign them."

"I agree."

Uncle Dan went to his bedroom and returned with a sock full of coins. He counted out the coins, then divided them in half and gave me my share. It totaled eight hundred dollars.

With my mother's blessing and Uncle Dan's agreement, I now needed to talk to just two more people. I went straight home after meeting with Uncle Dan to tell Daniel the news. After we celebrated with a glass of apple cider, the knots in my stomach returned. At first, I thought I'd put it off until to-morrow, but I was so excited I just couldn't wait any longer, so I lit a lantern and headed to Whitney's house.

I knocked on the front door, and Whitney's mother answered. She wel-comed me in, but instead, I asked if I could speak with Whitney outside. Whitney came out quickly and asked, "What's wrong?"

I was at a loss for words, but eventually I said, "Can you walk with me a spell? Do you remember a while back when Rev. Lee spoke at our church, and I asked you what you thought about Oregon, and would you ever con-sider leaving your family, knowing you might never see them again? Well, that's what I'm asking you now.

"I have loved you for a long time, and I think you care for me. I've decided I'm going to go to Oregon, and I'm going to leave next spring. I already have my mother's blessing and Uncle Dan's permission. All I need to know now is if you will join me.

"I know you're only sixteen now, but Daniel is going to come and join me in two years, and by then you will be eighteen. I want you to be my wife in Oregon. You can come with Daniel, and when you get there, we can be married."

"You know I love you, Thomas Merriman." she replied. "And if you're going to Oregon, I'm going to Oregon!

The only person left to talk to was Whitney's father. The lump in my throat doubled when I asked if I could talk to him. When he stepped outside, all of Whitney's brothers and sisters ran to the windows to hear what was going on. Whitney's mother shooed them away, and then she stepped outside to join us. With Whitney by my side, my courage returned, and I laid out the full plan for them. Then we waited for her father to speak. He said, "Two years is a long time. What if she changes her mind and decides she doesn't want to go to Oregon? Why not get married here before you leave, and she can go with you?"

My first thought was to say yes to his proposal, but then I thought better. It must be this way; I need time to prepare for Whitney's arrival. I have a house to erect, a sawmill to build, and this will be a dangerous journey. I love Whitney too much to ask her to come with me now. She must wait for my letters to know I'd made it, and I'm ready and waiting for her.

Whitney chimed in, please, Papa, say yes. He smiled at me and said, her mother and I will talk about it tonight and we will let you know tomorrow.

I left, feeling only half as happy as when I arrived.

It was the longest night of my life. I lay in bed waiting for the sunrise for what seemed like forever. When I did get up, I could hardly drink my cup of coffee. I put my boots on and headed to the mill just as the cock began to crow. I hooked up the horses and pulled a long piece of pine into the mill, then rolled it on to the cutting surface. I engaged the waterwheel and started the saw blade spinning. Before I began cutting the first slab off, I checked to see if anyone was coming. About halfway through the second cutting, I saw someone coming across the field, and my heart leaped; but it was only Uncle Dan. We stopped around nine o'clock to eat some biscuits Uncle had brought, but there was no sign of Whitney. My heart began to sink at the thought her father might say no. I had been so sure he would say yes. Mother and Uncle Dan had given their blessing, Daniel was going to join me; my plan was perfect.

By lunchtime, I had resigned myself to move forward without Whitney. Then, just when I was about to take my afternoon break, I saw the lumber wagon approaching with Whitney's father driving and Whitney sitting next to him. I began to run towards them but stopped, unsure if this meant the news was good or bad. I waited for what seemed like an eternity, when Whitney jumped down from the wagon and began running towards me, screaming, "Papa says yes, Papa says yes!"

You must have been happy, Mr. Merriman.

Call me Thomas.

I was walking on clouds, until I woke-up the next morning and realized how much I would need to accomplish before next spring.

Had you not given any thought about what it would take to go to Oregon?

I had. There had been a meeting in Independence, in conjunction with Rev. Lee's appearance to recruit people to join the Bidwell-Bartleson Party headed to Oregon and California the following spring. But it wasn't until then I realized how much preparation I needed to accomplish—no, that's not true, what really hit me was that I was leaving everyone I knew and loved behind, and I would more than likely never see them again! I realized I might not make it to Oregon, it was a long and treacherous journey; and even if I did, there was no guarantee Daniel and Whitney would!

Did you think about changing your mind?

No, I prayed about it, and God gave me peace.

So how does one prepare for the Oregon Trail?

The first thing I did was head to Independence to put my name on the list for the Bidwell-Bartleson Party headed to Oregon and California in the spring. Mr. Bidwell informed me the cost would be one dollar to join the party, and each member was to provide their own supplies. He then gave me a required list of food stuffs and hardware. He also explained the majority of the party would be heading to California, but that those wishing to go to Oregon would be able to find a guide when the party reached Fort Hall on the Snake River in the Idaho Country.

From about 1811 to 1840, the Oregon Trail was laid down by traders and fur trappers. It could be traveled only by horseback or on foot. By the year 1836, the first of the migrant train of wagons was put together. It started in Independence, Missouri, and traveled a cleared trail that reached to Fort Hall, Idaho. Work was done to clear more and more of the trail, stretching farther west, until it eventually reached the Willamette Valley, Oregon. Improvements on the trail in the form of better roads, ferries, bridges, and cutouts made the trip both safer and faster each year.

I was impressed by Mr. Bidwell; he was well spoken. I paid him one dollar, and he posted my name and my desired destination. I was the twelfth name on the list. My next stop was to go see Mr. Sowers again, but this time I brought money in the form of five- and ten-dollar gold pieces. I had Mr. Bidwell's list, besides one I had assembled myself, but I wanted Mr. Sowers to look over both lists and get his ideas. I explained to him my plans for setting up a sawmill in the Oregon Country and what I'd need to take with me to accomplish it. The thing I was most concerned about was the amount of weight my wagon would be carrying. Besides the components of the sawmill, food, and hardware, I needed to take a supply of lime and gypsum to create cement when I got there. We talked for nearly an hour and then agreed to meet the following week to discuss my options. I left him two ten-dollar gold pieces as a deposit.

Over the next week, I took exact measurements of the mill's waterwheel. Then I set about to duplicate each board, along with a blueprint for assembling the wheel once I reached Oregon.

I continued to work at the mill each day. Then Daniel, Whitney, and I spent nearly every night checking things off my lists, packing supplies, and making plans. Whitney and I talked a lot about the future. The one thing she wanted was to have a home with windows, so I had Mr. Sowers add two windows to my supplies.

When Mr. Sowers and I met again a week later, we began calculating the realistic cost of making the trip to Oregon. He said, "Your first choice has to be your form of transportation. You have two choices. The Conestoga wagon is eighteen feet long, four feet wide, and eleven feet high and can carry four to five people and twelve thousand pounds. There are several around here in good shape you can purchase for forty dollars or less. The other option is the prairie schooner, which is twelve to fifteen feet long, four feet wide, and ten feet tall and carries two people. It costs less, but it holds fewer supplies. Its advantage is it weighs only half of what a Conestoga wagon does, so it's easier to pull. Thus, fewer animals pulling equals less grain you'll have to take as feed.

> *Most movies and TV depict the pioneers using Conestoga wagons pulled by horses, with the pioneers riding. Actually, most pioneers used farm wagons called prairie schooners. They also walked the majority of the time instead of riding.*
>
> *Over the decades, as pioneers moved west, wagon technology improved, and wagons became lighter and more durable. Wagon manufacturing became one the leading industries in America during this period, and some of these companies are still operating today. The following are two companies that began as wagon manufacturers: John Deere and Sears and Roebuck.*

"Your second choice is what type of animal to choose to pull your wagon. The major choices are oxen or mules. The good news is, neither mules nor a yoke of oxen will be too hard to come by. You can buy a yoke of oxen for forty-five to fifty dollars, a set of mules even cheaper."

> *Most people chose mules. Unlike oxen, they responded to commands and training, and most importantly, they were cheap. Mules also learned their names and the tone and emotion in their driver's voice.*

"How much for a set of draft horses?" I asked.

"Draft horses will be at least double the cost of oxen, and we'll have to send for them from Kentucky. The horses will also cost more to feed.

"As for the required list of supplies you got from Bidwell and Bartleson: two hundred pounds of flour, one hundred fifty pounds of bacon, one hundred-pounds of rice, ten pounds of coffee, twenty pounds of sugar, ten pounds of salt, and one hundred pounds of beans, the cost will be $165 dollars. The cooking kettle, two frying pans, coffee pot, tin plates, cups, knives, and forks will be $35 dollars," Mr. Sowers said.

"To their list, I want to add a milk cow, a cock, four laying hens, and a long list of hardware items," I said. "I want to double the food stuffs as well. Once I get to Oregon, I will be busy building a home and the sawmill, and I don't want to worry about gathering food. I want two new rifles and a good supply of ammunition. I also want the best axes and a pair of both one-man and two-man handsaws.

"Once I reach Oregon, I will need draft horses and a wagon to haul logs to my mill and lumber to market, so I've decided I want the best pair draft horses available and the prairie schooner wagon," I said.

"Give me another week," Mr. Sowers said, "and I'll have a solid a cost for you."

I next went to see Mr. Beck the blacksmith to tell him my plan and to see if he could order me a set of tools of the trade I could take with me to Oregon.

I discussed my choices with Uncle Dan, and he agreed with my decisions about the draft horses and the wagon. He even came up with the idea of building a false floor in the wagon. "We can build a frame into the bed of the wagon and then cover it with wooden planks. This will allow you to place in it everything you will not need until you reach Oregon, like the sawmill components, the kegs of lime and nails, the wood for the waterwheel, and extra food stuffs, safely secured and out of the way of daily activities." I thought this would also be a safe place for Whitney's windows.

A few weeks later, Mr. Sowers sent word he needed to see me, so I set off for Independence. Upon arrival, I went directly to see him. When I walked through the hardware store's doors, I could see a large smile on his face as he said, "I've got great news." Then he walked me down to the livery stable where before me stood the most magnificent set of bay-colored draft horses I'd ever seen, six of them, their muscular structure and strength as evident as their slick shining coats of hair. Mr. Sowers said, "They are young but well trained. They just arrived in town a few days ago, and their owner wants to sell them. He also has a nearly new fifteen-foot wagon with water and flour barrels mounted on opposite sides. He wants three hundred dollars for everything, and that includes all the tack."

"Do you know why the owner wants to sell them?" I asked.

"He just bought a big spread several miles south of town, and he used six wagons to move his household supplies and slaves. He's decided to sell two of the wagons," Mr. Sowers said.

"I'll take the horses and wagon!" I said. "I'll bring the money by tomorrow."

Mr. Sowers also said, "I have determined the cost of the items on your lists. I can get you everything you've requested for five hundred dollars and have everything here within the next month."

"Thank you, Mr. Sowers," I said, "You've been a great help and a good friend."

Before I left town, I went by to see Mr. Bidwell. He informed me the list had grown to twenty men, and part of the new group included Father Pierre De Smet, his aide Father Nicholas Point, and Methodist preacher Joseph Williams; and at least half the group would now be headed to the Oregon Country.

I decided to share with Mr. Bidwell my list of additional items. He suggested eliminating most of them, especially since I was taking the sawmill items, which was going to add a considerable extra amount of weight. He said all my other items could be purchased from the Hudson's Bay Company once I reached Fort Vancouver. With this news, I decided to return to Mr. Sowers's store and cancel the purchase of the milk cow, cock, and chickens, as well as most of the extra food stuffs.

When I arrived at Mr. Sowers's store, he was busy with a customer, so I waited. The customer had a young black man with him. When he left, Mr. Sowers said, that's the man you're buying the horses and wagon from. I explained I had changed my mind about buying the milk cow and chickens, as well as the extra food items. He said that was fine. Then he said, wait till Yankee hears about this new fellow!

On my ride home, I began to think about how Yankee, as most people called him, was going to take the news: a new settler had moved into the county and had brought slaves with him. Yankee's real name was Humphrey Smith, and he hailed from New Jersey. He was the most outspoken opponent against slavery in Missouri, some said. Forced to move counties several times, he persisted in speaking his mind without concern for his own safety. I once heard him say, "Human slavery is a sin at all times and under all circumstances."

I remember asking my father about Yankee. I said, "Why do so many people hate him?"

He said, when someone speaks the truth and exposes evil, evil will always fight back. The Bible says God created man in his own image, and he loves us. The Bible doesn't say God created different races and made white people superior to all others. God loves all men and women; it's man who tries to claim superiority over others.

> *Prior to the United States buying the area known as the Louisiana Purchase in 1803, France, who owned it, had sanctioned slavery in the area. In 1812, the state of Louisiana, a major cotton producer and the first to be carved from the Louisiana Purchase, entered the Union as a slave state. Predictably, Missourians were adamant that slave labor should not be molested by the federal government. With Congress split over the issue of slavery and more slave owners moving into Missouri each year, the issue had reached the critical stage. A compromise was struck in 1820: Missouri would be admitted as a slave state and Maine as a free state.*

The next day, Daniel, Whitney, and I left early in the morning, money in hand, to buy our horses and wagon. We took the sawmill's wagon with a load of lumber to Independence. Daniel drove the sawmill's wagon back while Whitney and I stayed in town for a while, and we brought our new wagon back together. When we got back, we put the horses in the corral. I fed them and brushed them out. They were the first horses I'd ever owned, and I loved them—but not as much as I loved Whitney. I then walked Whitney home. Before we got to her house, she turned and kissed me, then ran up the porch. Today was a great day!

The next day, I oiled the canvas cover for the wagon and strung the wire hoops in preparation of sleeping in the wagon overnight. When I woke up the next morning, freezing, I added to my new list of supplies needed, four wool blankets. I can endure most things, but I hate being cold.

A few weeks later, Mr. Sowers sent word, some of my supplies had arrived, so I hooked up the wagon and went to collect my items. While in town, I checked the growing list of those headed to Oregon, but I also heard there was growing dissension among some about the leadership of the party, and a few were threatening to pull out of the group. A meeting of all interested parties was called for Sunday to discuss the issues openly.

The winter routine for the sawmill was logging, cutting down trees, and hauling them to the mill. While Daniel and Uncle Dan set off to work together, I went to another area by myself with my new draft horses. I had to prove to myself that for the next month I could fell trees, skid them to the mill, and cut lumber. If I could not, going to Oregon would be a complete failure. I was going to be on my own in the wilderness for nearly two years. I had to cut down trees, build a shelter, hunt and kill for meat, and plant vegetables, not to mention assemble a sawmill and construct a waterwheel.

This would be a daunting physical task and an even greater mental struggle. I needed to know before I left if I could accomplish it by myself. By the end of the first week, every muscle in my body burned with pain. It was clear I needed to practice my ax and saw skills; my lack of efficiency was requiring far too much physical exertion. I vowed to get up each morning thirty minutes earlier to practice until I left for Oregon.

Sunday morning, I traveled to Independence, where I proceeded to the meeting to hear the issues. I was surprised at the number of men there. The last time I had checked the list, there were only twenty men signed up; but there were well over thirty men in the hall. The issue, stated as clearly as possible, was the missionaries had hired the famous mountaineer Thomas "Broken Hand" Fitzpatrick to guide them to Oregon because of their concern over the lack of experience and leadership skills of John Bartleson. Mr. Bartleson had appointed himself as the leader, even calling himself Captain Bartleson, even though he was not nor had never been a military officer. He had never been west of the Mississippi River and was neither a trapper nor trader. On the other hand, Mr. Fitzpatrick had crossed the Rockies several times, hunted buffalo, traded with many of the western Indian tribes, and actually led parties west before.

> *Thomas Fitzpatrick (1799–1854), known as Broken Hand (reportedly because his left hand had been mangled in a firearms accident), was a famous mountain man, friend of the Native Americans, and trailblazer and trapper with the Rocky Mountain Fur Company. With Jedidiah Smith, he led a trapper band that discovered South Pass, Wyoming.*

My greatest fear was the rift would lead to a cancellation of the expedition if a compromise was not reached; but after a parlay between Fitzpatrick, Bartleson, Bidwell, and Father De Smet, an agreement was reached. Thomas Fitzpatrick would lead the party west until we reached the trail headed to California, at which point the two groups would split. Those headed to the Oregon Country would continue to be led by Mr. Fitzpatrick, while the group going to California would be led by Mr. Bartleson, who would keep his title of captain. The new cost would now be two dollars instead of one dollar. After the meeting concluded, another eight men signed up to go.

By mid-February, the soreness of my thirty-minute morning sessions was paying off. I was able to fell a tree in less time, more safely, and more efficiently. The next step in my transformation from a seventeen-year-old boy, nearly eighteen, to a trail-cutting, rugged explorer was learning how to cook. I had never cooked for myself; my mother, my aunt, or Whitney had always prepared my food. Now I would need to learn how to cook and, to make it more difficult, do it over an open fire. I decided starting tonight, I would cook myself supper with the pans and utensils I had just recently purchased.

By the time I got back to the house and fed and watered the horses, I had maybe thirty minutes of daylight left. I rushed to start a fire and get out my supplies. Everything was new and clean. They would never be the same again.

The first thing I did was fill the coffee pot with water, put in some grounds, and set it on a rock next to the fire. By this time, Daniel was home, and I invited him to join me for dinner. I got out the frying pans and placed a half dozen strips of bacon in one them. A few minutes later, I drained some the grease off from the bacon into another pan. I then put water into a cooking pot, added some beans, and placed them in the hot coals. Soon, the bacon was done, but the beans had yet to boil. When the beans did begin to boil, the water kept foaming up and boiling over the sides of the pot. After ten minutes of boiling, I dumped the beans into the pan with the bacon grease and stirred them, then I put them back in the fire. After a couple of minutes, I spooned half the beans on to a plate and handed the beans, bacon strips, and coffee to Daniel. I then dished up my own plate. The beans were burnt and hard, the bacon cold, and the coffee bitter.

That night was the last night Daniel ate with me for a while. As I lay awake, mostly due to indigestion, I began to rethink why I was going to Oregon. Not that I was having second doubts, but I began to question my real motivation. My first response was it was for God and country, what Rev. Lee called our destiny.

> *In the nineteenth century, manifest destiny was a belief that the United States would stretch from the Atlantic Ocean to the Pacific Ocean.*

But the more I thought about it, the more I dismissed patriotism as my real motivation. I began to consider thoughts I had not allowed myself to have for many years, thoughts I had hidden deeply in my mind, due to the pain I didn't want to acknowledge. The real reason I needed to do this was to give my life purpose and value. While to the outside world, it might not appear so, deep down inside, I felt abandoned, discarded, unwanted, and unloved.

After my father's death, my mother chose another man over Daniel and me. She gave us to my uncle's family, who provided for our physical needs; but we stood on the outside looking in, when it came to love and affection. The truth is, I needed to build a life that was mine and to have someone love me for who I was.

After three nights of horrible indigestion, I asked Whitney to teach me how to cook. The first thing she taught me was that beans have to soak overnight to be properly prepared. Next, she clued me in on the importance of cooking in the proper order, so food doesn't get cold or burn. Lastly, she had me add a little salt to the coffee to neutralize the bitterness. Together, we cooked supper for a week, by which time I was more confident of surviving the trip to Oregon. It was kind of like practicing for our future life together.

With each passing day, more pieces of the puzzle came together. The April 15 target date which once seemed so far away now approached faster than desired, and with each day my anxiety increased. I started to question myself—two years without seeing Daniel and Whitney. I'd never been lonely, but all of sudden I was lonely, and I hadn't even left yet.

To bide my time, I packed and unpacked, and each time, I discovered something I didn't have or of which I didn't have enough. Today it was candles, salt, and reading materials. On my next trip to town, I ordered three more boxes of candles and another five pounds of salt. I had my fiddle to keep me company, but I felt compelled to bring something to read. I stopped by Mother's to ask if I could have the family Bible. I think the request startled her with the realization I was actually leaving, and she was overcome with emotion. She held me for a long time, then tearfully retreated and returned with the Bible. We held each other again with great feeling before I left.

On the way home, I stopped at an orchard and cut starts off two types of apple trees, a pear tree, and a peach tree. I then pushed each start into a potato and wrapped them in a burlap bag. If everything went as planned, I could plant them once I reached Oregon, and within a few years, I'd have fruit trees of my own.

Upon returning with our family Bible, I shared my desire with Whitney of taking some books to read. She surprised me a few days later with two books, *The Legend of Sleepy Hollow* and the complete book of *Grimms' Fairy Tales*. In the weeks before I left, we read them together. With the days running short, I tried spending as much time as I could spare with Whitney, but as the time approached the appointed day to leave, the feelings of abandonment arose in my heart again, not of being abandoned personally but of abandoning someone I loved.

As I packed everything for the last time, my body began to tremble, my heart was racing, and I could hardly speak without my voice faltering It was time to say my goodbyes to people I'd known my whole life but would more than likely never see again. In the end, I hugged and kissed most but could not find words that expressed my feelings to any. As a goodbye gift, Whitney's mother gave me a box of preserves and a quilt she had made; Aunt Rose gave me a tin of dried venison and a box of oatmeal cookies. Uncle Dan had tears in his eyes as he shook my hand and said, "Your father would be very proud of you!"

The last goodbyes were reserved for Daniel and Whitney. I hugged Daniel, then I kissed Whitney goodbye. It was the hardest thing I'd ever done. As I mounted my wagon, I told them I'd write along the way and as soon as I got there to let them know my location. I'd already said my goodbyes to my sisters and Mother a few days earlier, but as I made my way to Independence by myself, tears started streaming down my face. then I began bawling so hard I had to stop the wagon to gain composure before I continued.

*We call those who settled the West **pioneers**. The word is derived* *from the Latin word **pedonem**, which means "one who goes on foot." It was first applied to foot soldiers in the army. The word eventually came to mean one of lower social status, such as an infantry soldier or labor. The evolved word for this was **peon**. In French, it came to mean agricultural worker or one who clears land; and because of its use during the eighteenth-century wars, **pionnier** meant units that "go first" to prepare the path for a "larger army."*

Once I reached Independence, a new emotion came over me, one of excitement and anticipation of the unknown. I felt like a child learning to walk and craving to run. By the time I reached the designated site, there were already nine wagons in line. I became number ten. Within a few hours, our new Corps of Discovery had reached fifteen wagons and seventy men plus women and children. Mr. Bidwell was checking people in and inspecting the tar covering the sides and belly of their wagons. He pointed out, "The streams and rivers we will be crossing will often be as high as the top of your wagon's wheels, and if you want to keep the items in your wagon dry, you must keep your wagon well tarred. It is best to keep a tar bucket mounted on the outside of your wagon and to check every day to make sure the travel and heat have not caused any cracks." Having packed items such as lime, extra salt, and other valuables in the bottom of my wagon, I inspected my wagon thoroughly and then applied another coat of tar to several areas.

As the sun began to set, Thomas Fitzpatrick called a meeting. He explained, "We will have a wake-up shot at 4 a.m. You will have one hour to prepare your breakfast and lunch and to be packed and ready to go. We will stop for lunch after four hours or so and will start again around 2 p.m. We will stop each night around 6 p.m. Starting tomorrow night, we will establish a rotating list of men to stand guard during the night, and they will also fire off the wake-up shot. We will try to camp each night near fresh water and grass for the animals, but that will not always be possible, so keep your water barrels full. We will travel twelve to fifteen miles each day. It is important to keep your animals as fresh and strong as possible, so you will need to walk and lead your teams. Do not ride in your wagons unless absolutely necessary. Once we cross the Missouri River, there will be no turning back, so get a good night's sleep; tomorrow will be a big day."

Before we turned in for the night, Father De Smet prayed for safe passage, good health, calm heads, and loving hearts. Not being Catholic, I wasn't entirely comfortable with Father De Semt praying for me, so before I closed my eyes, I prayed the Lord would watch over us and keep Daniel and Whitney safe as well.

That must have been a great day, to know you had accomplished all your preparation, and in just a few hours you would start off on your adventure.

Before I end our first interview session, I'd like to ask a few questions.

Obviously, you put a great deal of time and effort into the planning of this journey. Was there anything you forgot, or it turned out you really didn't need like you thought you would?

If had to do it again, I would definitely have brought more socks and boots. I never thought about the need for extra footwear, and no one else mentioned it. But walking every day took an extreme toll on my feet. Most of the time they were sweating. Other times, after crossing rivers, my boots and socks were soaked, as I trudged on for miles or until we stopped for the evening and I could remove them. My feet seemed as if they were either blistered, wrinkled, or cracked, for the first month of the trip. They called us "tenderfoots." Looking back, I would have brought two extra pairs of boots and two dozen more pairs of socks.

Was there anything it turned out you didn't need?

No, sooner or later, I pretty well used everything I brought.

You said, after listening to Rev. Lee, you dreamed of nothing but huge evergreen trees and sawmill blades cutting lumber. Did any of the other things Mr. Lee spoke of factor into your decision to leave Missouri and move to Oregon?

I understood both England and the U.S. claimed they owned the Oregon Country, and whoever had the greater claim would more than likely come down to which country had the largest number of citizens living there. But I think, for me, it was more about the opportunities and the adventure.

I found it interesting that your father and his brother left West Virginia to move to Missouri, for greater opportunities. Then, you and your brother left Missouri for Oregon, for the same reasons. Did you think about your father's choice when you were making your decision?

I thought about my father very much, and I wished I could ask him his opinion on whether I should go or stay. I've always believed he would have said, go!

I would like to talk about your Oregon Trail experiences the next time we meet, if that's OK with you.

I'll do you one better. I kept a journal of the journey, writing my thoughts and experiences down nearly every day. I sent it back in sections to Daniel and Whitney in Missouri, so they could read it before they left. They returned the full journal to me when they arrived. Now, I will give it to you!

CHAPTER 2

Leaving Missouri Behind, 1841
First Leg of the Trail

You can learn a great deal from a diary. People tend to write down more than just the facts; they write down their interpretation of the facts. Therefore, when you read a diary, remember you are looking at the events through their eyes. Another person living through the same events may have a totally different interpretation. A good example of such a case would be the men of the Lewis and Clark expedition. Lewis, Clark, and a number of other members of the Corps of Discovery published their journals. Having read them all, you might conclude they must have taken separate trips.

I have tried to let Mr. Merriman's words speak for themselves. I have corrected his spelling and grammar and have a few times interpreted his writing and filled in the blanks. He wrote something down nearly every day—sometimes in the morning, other times in the evening, some days both.

May 9, 1841 (evening)

The first leg of our journey will take us from Independence, Missouri, to the Great Platte River Trail, approximately two hundred miles or twelve to fourteen days.

Day 1, May 10, Monday (evening)

It was biscuits and jam for breakfast. Up an hour before dawn, I prepared breakfast and lunch, ate, and readied my wagon to travel. The sunrise was joyous. I felt alert and ready to start the journey I had been planning for months, praying about for years. A shotgun blast signaled we were leaving, and each wagon fell into line. I was in the middle of the pack, and I tried to take in all the fanfare. There were hundreds of well-wishers applauding our parade of wagons. Women and young children, dressed in their Sunday best, walked beside their wagons, waving flags and shouting farewells to family and friends.

> *The first part of what would become the Oregon Trail followed the Santa Fe Trail. Established in the early 1800s, the trail was first used by smugglers who traded supplies with Mexican outposts. After Mexico's independence from Spain, trade became legal, and the Santa Fe Trail became a major course of commerce. While the trail was well used, it was not easily traveled.*

By midday, all wagons had crossed the Missouri River and all celebration had vanished, as reality set in. We hadn't completed one day's journey, and you could hear voices complaining, "Can't we slow down, I'm tired, can we take a break, my feet hurt, my stomach is churning, I'm going to be sick." Fitzpatrick called them tenderfoots and greenhorns. For those who were not used to walking long distances, fifteen to twenty miles is a long, arduous, physically exhausting daily trek. Bad shoes caused blisters and sores. Riding across the uneven landscape caused the wagons to rock back and forth, causing those riding to suffer from motion sickness.

> *The Missouri River originates in the Rocky Mountains and flows east until it reaches the Mississippi River.*

When we reached our first day's destination, the wagon train formed a large circle, and all the horses, oxen, and other cattle were herded into the center before the last few wagons closed up the circle. This provided a safe area, easily defended against wild animals, as well as a place for the animals to eat and rest for the night. Personal campfires were built on the outside of the wagon circle for further protection and for preparing food.

People I associated with today: Richard and Lizzie Williams, one son, one daughter. Ben Kelsey and wife and child. Sam Kelsey (Ben's brother), wife and two children. Andy Kelsey (single). Betsey Gray (Ben's wife's sister), one child, no husband. Zaid (no last name), married to Martha's older sister Winnie. Preacher Williams. John Bidwell.

What I learned today:

River crossings are very dangerous during the spring runoff.

Each party usually establishes its own rules. They typically include rules for departure, traveling, camp setup, behavior, treatment of the sick and ill, and disposition of the property of deceased members.

Some trains stop every Sunday, while others hold brief church services and then push forward in the afternoon. Days of rest are planned more for the benefit of animals than humans. Activities on days off usually include making needed repairs to wagons, doing the laundry, and socializing.

Weather-related dangers include thunderstorms, lethally large hailstones, lightning, tornadoes, and high winds.

Day 2, May 11, Tuesday (morning)

If the first day tested the physical strength of the party, the first evening tested our patience. After securing my wagon and animals, searching for firewood and preparing the evening meal became my next priority. Within a few hours, the sun had set, and the stars and moon replaced the sunlight. However, with the nocturnal hours, came the sounds and rustling of wild creatures that caused the party's dogs to go into a frenzy that lasted all night long. I might have slept an hour, if that, before a shotgun blast signaled it was time to awake and rise.

Day 2, May 11 (evening)

Today was more of the same, traversing the flat grassland. In some places, the grass was waist high. I had to climb up onto the back of one of my horses to get an idea of where we were headed. The Great Plains stretched as far as I could see, and it seemed as if God had forgotten to plant trees in this ocean of grass. When the wind blew, it was like watching waves breaking and receding on a distant shore.

One of the party's members, a greenhorn, struggling with keeping his young oxen in line, lost control of his wagon and Broken Hand Fitzpatrick had to rescue the greenhorn and his wagon from certain destruction. For the rest of the day, Fitzpatrick rode alongside the greenhorn's team of oxen, and each time they began to act up, he pelted the oxen with stones. By the end of the day, the oxen were more responsive to the greenhorn's commands.

If the first day was tough on the greenhorns and tenderfoots, the second day was worse. All I could think was, who in their right mind tackles such a physically taxing journey with such ill-prepared minds, bodies, and souls.

It was another night of howling coyotes, wolves, and dogs.

What I learned today:

Intense heat causes wood to shrink, and wagon wheels need to be soaked in water at night or whenever possible, to keep their iron rims from rolling right off during the day. The heat also takes a toll on the horses' and oxen's feet: their shoes fall off, and their hooves split. To cure this, you treat their hooves with tar.

Blistered lips are a common problem. Mine are blistered. I was told to smear axle grease on them.

Stampedes of buffalo are a concern. They can tip over wagons, trample people, and scatter livestock.

Day 3, May 12, Wednesday (morning)

Sleep came quickly to me last night, my having hardly slept the night before. The morning brought more dissension within the party's ranks between those who owned dogs and those angry about their constant barking. It was clear nerves were nearing the breaking point for many, and we had barely learned each other's names.

People I associated with today: Richard and Lizzie Williams, Preacher Williams, and John Bidwell.

Day 3, May 12 (evening)

North wind blowing hard, going to be a cold night with snow flurries, Fitzpatrick said. He announced we had covered, in his estimation, 32 miles in the first two days. He then informed us, we had 178 miles more before we reached the location of where several trails joined together into a single trail known as the Great Platte River Trail, where we would take our first scheduled day off.

Today we passed by what is the first of many landmarks on the trail. It's known as Big Blue, a large sandstone mound. Just before noon, I could begin to make out the unusual land formation rising from the flat grasslands. I noticed others were pointing to it as well. As we continued to travel, the rock formation grew in proportion to the horizon, and clearly, it had a blue-hued coloration. As we reached its base, the wagon train came to a halt. Members of the party stopped their wagons and began climbing to the top of the formation. It was so out of place, this blue mound in an area flat as the eye could see. I stopped, staked my team and wagon, then followed the others to the top. It looked as if I could see forty miles ahead. Soon, I could hear Fitzpatrick yelling we must keep moving.

As we started again, Fitzpatrick announced tonight we would camp at a water hole where people could wash up and bathe but only after everyone had filled their water supply and watered their animals. He cautioned everyone to make sure they kept all animals away from the spring so as to not contaminate it. "There is no cure for cholera," he shouted.

> Cholera is an infectious disease that causes severe watery diarrhea, which can lead to dehydration and even death, if untreated. It is caused by eating food or drinking water contaminated with a bacterium called **vibrio cholerae**.

After a few more hours on the trail, we saw our first herd of buffalo. From a distance, the ground appeared to be a sea of black, but as we approached, I could see individual cows, calves, and bulls. We passed to the outside of the herd without occasion. The buffalo seemed to have no concern or interest in our movement. There was a discussion about whether we should shoot one for the meat, but Fitzpatrick explained there would be plenty of opportunities later, when our supplies where shorter and our wagons weighed less.

Upon reaching our evening's destination, I secured my wagon and cared for my horses. I gathered a small amount of firewood and began filling my water barrel. Betsey Gray was also getting water, so we talked as we made trips back and forth to the watering hole.

I began to prepare my supper, when I decided it could wait until I took a swim. It felt great to wash three day's dust off my body, and the cool water felt good on my sore leg muscles. The break also gave me my first real opportunity to visit with other fellow party members. When I reached the water hole, Father De Smet was already bathing. We struck up a conversation about his travels and his mission to spread the gospel to the Indians. I asked if he enjoyed working with the Indian tribes. "I do," he said. "For the most part, they are very friendly people."

"Now, conversion is another issue," he said. "They all tend to practice a form of religion known as animism; they worship different animals they believe have godlike powers. Some of the biggest problems are the lack of a written language and their refusal to give up previous beliefs and traditions. One of the largest conflicts has been over the belief of monogamous marriages; it is very common for Indian men to have several wives. It doesn't help that many of the fur traders and trappers engage with many Indian women promiscuously outside of marriage. The one positive thing the Indians do enjoy is our Catholic ceremonies and rituals." Before he left, he invited me to come to his first Sunday sermon. He said, "I'm going to be speaking about Shadrach, Meshach, and Abednego."

> *Animism is the belief held by many indigenous people that all things are alive and possess a spiritual essence.*

What I learned today:

Cholera is the most feared disease: people can be in good spirits in the morning, in agony by noon, and dead by evening. The symptoms start with a stomachache, followed by intense pain, diarrhea, and vomiting. Your skin begins to wrinkle and turn blue. It you don't die within twenty-four hours, you usually recover.

Accidents are usually caused by negligence, exhaustion, guns, animals, and the weather.

Day 4, May 13, Thursday (morning)

It was another sleepless night, with dogs barking until nearly sunrise. I overheard a threat from one man: if the owners of the dogs could not keep them quiet, he would personally take care of the issue himself. I knew this was a powder keg ready to explode. I tried to think of ways I could prevent this showdown before cooler heads could prevail. I finally decided it would be a good night to get out my fiddle and let everyone relax and get to know each other a little better, and there is no better way than with a little music.

Day 4, May 13 (evening)

After traveling for several hours, I could see a commotion ahead of me, so I pulled my horses up short, staked them quickly, and ran forward to the trouble.

When I reached the crowd of onlookers, I asked what had happened. I could see a small child was lying on the ground. The man next to me said she had apparently fallen asleep and fallen off the wagon, and one of the wagon wheels had rolled over her leg. Before I could move, someone began shouting, does anyone have a short board and some swaddling; her leg is broken. I went to get a board from my wagon and returned. I gave the woman a board and off she ran. After an hour's delay, we began moving again. The incident pointed out the frailty of our situation. Going forward, there would be no medical help until we reached Fort Laramie, which would be another seven weeks, give or take a little.

The little girl's accident brought the wagon train closer together and defused the barking dog conflict. Everyone rallied together to support the young child and her family. I decided to keep the fiddle in its case; it didn't seem like the right moment for a night of music. As all members of our small troop gathered around a common campfire visiting, the woman who had taken the board from me introduced herself as Mary, then said, this is my husband, Sam. I had seen them before, but it was the first time I had interacted with the majority of my fellow travelers. I enjoyed talking with Mary and Sam. They're nice people. I'm going to try and get to know them better.

Day 5, May 14, Friday (morning)

It may have been the excitement from yesterday's activities, but I lay in my makeshift bed last night for hours without falling asleep. The good news, the dogs didn't seem to bark too much.

What I learned from yesterday:

The accident ratified to me, we are all alone out here in the wilderness, and we have no one but ourselves for support.

Day 5, May 14 (evening)

Today, we crossed the Kansas River, turned north, and began to parallel the Little Blue River, which flows in a north/northwest direction. While the river was in sight all day, we did not follow its meandering path but instead followed a narrow, unwavering, straight trail. Boredom has set in; it's more of the same, grasslands stretching as far as the eye can see, more of placing one foot in front of the other for hours on end. By the end of the day, we had put another twenty miles behind us, yet it was hard to tell we had even moved. Tonight's campsite looked just like the one we had the night before, and the view ahead looked the same as today's.

Day 6, May 15, Saturday (morning)

The trouble began first thing. I could hear three men arguing with another man. Soon others arrived, and the yelling became louder and the threats stronger, but before it came to fisticuffs or worse, Mr. Bidwell took charge. He told everyone to be ready to move out within the hour; we would decide this issue this evening before we retire for the night.

I put some grease on my wagon wheel's axels and my lips before we moved out.

Day 6, May 15 (evening)

We met after supper as a group. Mr. Bidwell acted as the moderator. The major issue was dogs barking all night and the lack of sleep. Bidwell suggested we bring whatever choices we discuss to a vote, and everyone, men and women, would have one vote—the majority would rule—to which all agreed. It was very clear the issue of dogs barking all night had reached a breaking point, and the group was split, those with dogs and those without. It was also very clear those with dogs were in the minority. They argued the dogs were needed to help protect the other animals and were a first line of defense against Indians. But in the end, the majority voted to kill all dogs that continuously barked. Tonight, three dogs were shot!

Day 7, May 16, Sunday (morning)

Very quiet morning, everyone keeping to themselves. There were definitely several people very upset about the loss of their animals. Last night, I had a very vivid dream. I saw myself walking along a clear, flowing river on a narrow trail, under towering trees that seemed to touch the sky like mountains. Next, I was standing in an open field and walking towards a log house. I could see a young woman and two children standing outside, and then I woke up.

Day 7, May 16 (evening)

We had good traveling today, covered an extra mile or two, but as the evening progressed, the wind began to blow and dark clouds quickly filled the sky. Those intent on killing all dogs were ready with guns loaded, and with the first barking, I heard two shots. But as the group moved towards a third target, screaming could be heard by all. I rushed towards the commotion. Mr. Anderson and his eldest son had their shotguns drawn and cocked, as Mrs. Anderson held their two dogs. Mr. Anderson continuously repeated he would kill anyone who shot his dogs. The standoff lasted only a few more seconds before both Mr. Bidwell and Mr. Bartleson arrived and defused the situation. They made it clear no more dogs were going to be shot tonight and everyone was to return to their wagons immediately! They then posted an extra man on duty for the remainder of the night, near the Anderson's wagon.

Day 8, May 17, Monday (morning)

A violent rainstorm broke out during the night and kept me awake. I had washed most of my clothes on Sunday and laid them out to dry overnight; they were completely soaked. To complicate the morning's other problems, several members of the party came to Bidwell to say they had changed their mind about the killing of all dogs for barking. Bidwell called a quick meeting and announced the killing of dogs no longer would take place—although it was clear there was still resentment towards the Andersons. We covered only about twelve miles today.

Day 9, May 18, Tuesday (evening)

No rain today. The sun's warmth dried things out. After taking care of my animals, I built a fire and completed the drying process of my bedding. Tonight, we actually camped by the river's side. The running stream brought sleep quickly.

Day 10, May 19, Wednesday (morning)

As everyone readied for the day's travel, word circulated that one family had a sick child and were asking the wagon train to wait another day before leaving. Bidwell and Bartleson met with the young couple and told them the train would not wait but would continue forward. They told them the trail between here and the Great Platte River Trail can be easily followed; just keep the river in sight.

The ready signal was given, and soon we were on our way. We were told they would follow when the child felt better. It was a very clear message, the train stops for no one. It was also circulated, within a few days, we would reach the point of no return. It would be the last chance for stragglers and those with second thoughts to return back to Missouri.

Day 11, May 20, Thursday (evening).

Fitzpatrick says we are three days from the start of the Great Platte River Trail.

> *This site would eventually become known as Fort Kearny. In 1838, Colonel Stephen W. Kearny scouted the area along the Missouri River at the mouth of Table Creek near present-day Nebraska City, looking for a suitable location for an outpost to protect westward travelers. In 1846, following Kearny's recommendation, the United States War Department ordered the building of an outpost on the site and directed Kearny to construct one there.*

Day 12, May 21, Friday (evening)

We sighted a large herd of buffalo today. It was decided we would stop and kill a couple of yearlings. Meat was divided equally among the party. It was decided we would have a group barbeque on Sunday. The Jordan family, whom we had left behind earlier in the week, pulled into camp in the late afternoon. Fitzpatrick checked the family's health, then agreed they could continue with the wagon train.

Day 13, May 22, Saturday (morning)

Fitzpatrick said we will be at the beginning of the Great Platte River Trail by midafternoon, and tomorrow would be a day of rest.

Day 13, May 22 (evening)

We reached the Great Platte River Trail midafternoon, just as Fitzpatrick said we would. After caring for my horses and wagon, I began gathering firewood for myself and extra, so we could begin cooking our buffalo meat. Looking forward to Father De Smet's sermon tomorrow!

Day 14, May 23, Sunday (morning)

No gun shot as a wake-up call today, yet I woke up early! Put on my best clothes for church services. Most of the party showed up to hear Father De Smet's message.

Father De Smet opened the service with prayer. He then began, "I thought I'd share the story of Shadrach, Meshach, and Abednego with you this Sunday. Three young men who placed their trust in God, over expediency.

"After the Israelites were defeated by King Nebuchadnezzar, many of Israel's people were forced into slavery and deported to Babylon, the capital of Nebuchadnezzar's empire. Three of these Hebrews proved to be skilled and wise, finding favor with the king—until Nebuchadnezzar had an image of gold made of his likeness and summoned all his provincial officials to come to the dedication of his image.

"Here it was proclaimed, 'Nations and peoples of every language, you are commanded: As soon as you hear the sound of the horn, flute, zither, lyre, harp, pipe, and all other kinds of music, to fall down and worship the golden image of King Nebuchadnezzar. Whoever does not fall down and worship will immediately be thrown into a blazing furnace.'

"Soon, some astrologers came forward and said to King Nebuchadnezzar, 'May the King live forever! Your Majesty has issued a decree that everyone who hears the sound of the horn, flute, zither, lyre, harp, pipe, and all kinds of music must fall down and worship your image of gold, and whoever does not fall down and worship will be thrown into a blazing furnace. There are some Jews (Shadrach, Meshach, and Abednego) who pay no attention to you, Your Majesty. They neither serve your gods nor worship your image of gold.'

"Furious with rage, Nebuchadnezzar summoned Shadrach, Meshach, and Abednego. The three men were brought before the king, and Nebuchadnezzar said to them, is it true, you do not serve my gods or worship my image of gold? To which they replied, yes! Furious, the king said, 'I will give you one more chance, but if you do not worship my golden image, you will be thrown immediately into a blazing furnace. Then what god will be able to rescue you from my hand?'

"Shadrach, Meshach, and Abednego replied to him, 'King Nebuchadnezzar, we do not need to defend ourselves before you in this matter. If we are thrown into the blazing furnace, the god we serve is able to deliver us from it, and he will deliver us from Your Majesty's hand. But even if he does not, we want you to know, Your Majesty, we will not serve your gods or worship your image of gold.'

"Nebuchadnezzar's heart was filled with rage towards Shadrach, Meshach, and Abednego, and he ordered the furnace heated seven times hotter than usual and commanded the strongest soldiers in his army to tie up Shadrach, Meshach, and Abednego and throw them into the blazing furnace. The furnace was so hot, the flames of the fire killed the soldiers.

"Then King Nebuchadnezzar leaped to his feet in amazement and asked his advisers, 'Weren't there three men whom we tied up and threw into the fire?'

"They replied, 'Certainly, Your Majesty.'

"He said, 'Look! I see four men walking around in the fire, unbound and unharmed, and the fourth looks like a son of the gods.'

"Nebuchadnezzar then approached the opening of the blazing furnace and shouted, 'Shadrach, Meshach, and Abednego, servants of the Most High God, come out! Come here!

"Shadrach, Meshach and Abednego came out of the fire, and the royal advisers crowded around them. They saw the fire had not harmed their bodies, nor was a hair of their heads singed; their robes were not scorched, and there was no smell of fire on them.

"Then Nebuchadnezzar said, 'Praise be to the god of Shadrach, Meshach, and Abednego, who has sent his angel and rescued his servants! They trusted in him and defied the king's command and were willing to give up their lives rather than serve or worship any god except their own god. Therefore, I decree that the people of any nation or language who say anything against the god of Shadrach, Meshach, and Abednego be cut into pieces and their houses be turned into piles of rubble, for no other god can save in this way.'

"Then the king promoted Shadrach, Meshach, and Abednego in the province of Babylon.

"This story, along with Daniel and the lions' den, are found in the book of Daniel. Both teach us that if we place our faith in the one true God, he will deliver us. As far as I know, there are no lions between here and Oregon, or any fiery furnaces, but I do know there will be trials and tribulations on our travels, and I'm sure even after you arrive at your destinations. I encourage you to put your faith in the God of Shadrach, Meshach, and Abednego as you walk each day, and if you do, He promises He will be there beside you."

The remainder of the day was filled with rest and food—barbequed buffalo, to be exact. It was a time to get to know everyone better. There was a horseshoe tournament. My partner and I finished in second place. In the evening, those of us heading to Oregon visited by ourselves. This was our first real opportunity to get to know each other. While I enjoyed visiting with everyone, I feel I have found kindred spirits in Sam and Mary. I ended the evening by taking out my fiddle and playing a few tunes.

Day 15, May 24, Monday (morning)

Today we start our second leg, along the Platte River.

The Platte River is a major river in the state of Nebraska and is about

> *310 miles long. The Platte, over most of its length, is a muddy, broad, shallow, meandering stream with a swampy bottom. The river valley played an important role in the westward expansion of the United States, providing the route for several major emigrant trails, including the Oregon, California, Mormon, and Bozeman Trails. The first Europeans to see the Platte were French explorers and fur trappers about 1714; they first called it the Nebraskier (Nebraska), a transliteration of the name given by the Otoe people, meaning "flat water." This expression is very close to the French words **rivière plate** ("flat river"), the probable origin of the name Platte River.*

Day 16, May 25, Tuesday (evening)

Day 1 of traveling across Grand Island, which is well wooded. Believe it or not, this island is supposedly fifty miles long. Huge mosquitoes. Most of us have numerous bites that itch terribly.

Day 17, May 26, Wednesday (evening)

Day 2 on Grand Island, flat, easy travel, covered twenty miles. In the afternoon, we stopped at a watering hole (a large spring) to let the animals drink and for the party to fill their water barrels. While we rested, I watched large birds fly overhead. They swooped and soared on the hot air currents.

Day 18, May 27, Thursday (evening)

Day 3 on Grand Island. We have reached the end of the island. Tomorrow, we will cross to the main land and continue our journey west. Mosquitoes still a problem, and the area seems to be the home to a large variety of snakes. I hate snakes!

Day 19, May 28, Friday (evening)

I spent time by myself after our journey today, giving extra attention to my horses and wagon. The horses and I have developed a special bond. I can see it in their eyes, and I'm sure they can see it in mine. Wagon is in good shape, its contents dry and intact.

Day 20, May 29, Saturday (evening)

Tonight I have guard duty. My thoughts center around Whitney wondering what her day we like and did she miss me as much as I miss her.

Day 21, May 30, Sunday (evening)

Had dinner with Sam and Mary. I asked them why they had decided to move to Oregon. They said they wanted a new beginning, and Oregon seemed like the best place to do that. In Missouri, they were share croppers, people who don't own the land they work but split the profits with the land-owner. They said, "For the past three years, we've put our hearts and backs into growing cotton. Last year, we made a stake, and we decided to invest it by going to Oregon, where we can farm our own land."

I asked them what they intended to do once they got there. Mary said, "We plan to make a land claim, build a home, and raise our family."

I asked what was their plan, as far as income. They said they were trusting God to provide an opportunity.

They asked me about my plans, and I shared I was going to set up a sawmill, and my brother and fiancée would be making the trip to Oregon next year to join me. I thanked Mary for dinner—she's a good cook! I invited them to dine with me next time.

Day 22, May 31, Monday (morning)

Giving a lot of thought about asking Sam if he would like to be a partner in the sawmill. With Daniel's, mine, and Sam's land claims, we could have more trees than we could use in a lifetime.

Day 23, June 1, Tuesday (evening)

The grass along the river has turned to short prairie grass. There are very few trees for wood, so we are now using buffalo dung as fuel for our fires.

Day 24, June 2, Wednesday (morning)

I had the dream again. I was walking towards a log house, I could see a young woman, and this time I recognized her.

Day 24, June 2 (evening)

Most people spent the morning giving extra attention to their animals and wagons. Sam and Mary stopped by for a visit and invited me to have supper with them.

Day 25, June 3, Thursday (evening)

Dissension in camp, some people hoarding firewood, which is in short supply.

Day 26, June 4, Friday (morning)

Rained last night. Francis trying to make fire this morning, using wet wood, thought he could help the matter by sprinkling some powder from his powder horn over the small blaze. The powder horn exploded, he ran to the creek and bathed his hands and face, came back destitute of whiskers and eyebrows.

Day 27, June 5, Saturday (morning)

Finally, a morning with blue sky and no threat of rain today!

Day 28, June 6, Sunday (evening)

No travel today. After breakfast, I put on my best clothes and gathered with the majority of the party to worship God. I brought my fiddle and accompanied another member playing the accordion. We played a few hymns before Father De Smet began reading from the Bible the story of Daniel in the den of lions.

"Now King Darius of Persia appointed administrators to help him rule over his kingdom, one of whom was Daniel. The administrators were made accountable so that the king might not suffer loss. Daniel so distinguished himself among all the administrators by his exceptional qualities that the king planned to set him over the whole kingdom. Jealous, the other administrators tried to find grounds for charges against Daniel in his conduct of government affairs, but they were unable to do so. They could find no corruption in him, because he was trustworthy and neither corrupt nor negligent. Finally, these men said, 'We will never find any basis for charges against this man Daniel unless it has something to do with the law of his God.'

"So, these administrators as a group went to the king and said: 'May King Darius live forever!' They convinced the king he should issue an edict and enforce the decree that anyone who prays to any god or human being other than the king during the next thirty days shall be thrown into the lions' den. They not only convinced King Darius to make the decree but to put it in writing so it could not be altered—in accordance with the law of the Medes and Persians.

> The Medes and Persians were two Iranian peoples who were united under Cyrus the Great.

"When Daniel learned the decree had been published, he went home to his upstairs room where the windows opened toward Jerusalem and prayed. Three times a day, he got down on his knees and prayed, giving thanks to his god, just as he had done before. Then these men went as a group and found Daniel praying and asking God for help. They then went to the king and spoke to him about his royal decree: 'Did you not publish a decree that during the next thirty days anyone who prays to any god or human, except to you, would be thrown into the lions' den?'

"The king answered, 'The decree stands—in accordance with the law of the Medes and Persians, which cannot be repealed.'

"Then they said to the king, 'Daniel, who is one of the exiles from Judah, pays no attention to you, Your Majesty, or to the decree you put in writing. He still prays three times a day.' When the king heard this, he was greatly distressed; he was determined to rescue Daniel and made every effort until sundown to save him.

"Then the men went as a group to King Darius and said to him, "Remember, Your Majesty, that according to the law of the Medes and Persians, no decree or edict that the king issues can be changed.'

"So, the king gave the order, and they brought Daniel and threw him into the lions' den. The king said to Daniel, 'May your god, whom you serve continually, rescue you!'

"A stone was brought and placed over the mouth of the den, and the king sealed it with his own signet ring, so that Daniel's situation might not be changed. Then the king returned to his palace and spent the night without eating and without any entertainment being brought to him. And he could not sleep.

"At the first light of dawn, the king got up and hurried to the lions' den. When he came near the den, he called to Daniel in an anguished voice, 'Daniel, servant of the living god, has your god, whom you serve continually, been able to rescue you from the lions?'

"Daniel answered, 'May the king live forever! My god sent his angel, and he shut the mouths of the lions. They have not hurt me, because I was found innocent in his sight. Nor have I ever done any wrong before you, Your Majesty.'

"The king was overjoyed and gave orders to lift Daniel out of the den. And when Daniel was lifted from the den, no wound was found on him, because he had trusted in his god.

"At the king's command, the men who had falsely accused Daniel were brought in and thrown into the lions' den, along with their wives and children. And before they reached the floor of the den, the lions overpowered them and crushed all their bones.

"Then King Darius wrote to all the nations and peoples of every language in all the earth:

"'May you prosper greatly!

"'I issue a decree that in every part of my kingdom, people must fear and reverence the god of Daniel.

"'For he is the living god and he endures forever; his kingdom will not be destroyed, his dominion will never end. He rescues and he saves; he performs signs and wonders in the heavens and on the earth. He has rescued Daniel from the power of the lions.'"

After Sunday services, Betsey Gray asked if I would like to accompany her on a picnic. Mary overheard the invitation and quickly suggested Betsey, her son, and I join their family for afternoon super. My first thought was Mary's invitation was rude, since Betsey had already extended her invitation; but after Betsey left, Mary explained that "picnic" was a code word for married couples to slip off to a private spot for marital relations. "If you had gone," she said, "they would have had you married to her within a week, no matter what took place."

Day 29, June 7, Monday (morning)

We reached where the Platte River splits into two forks, now following North Fork of the Platte River.

Day 30, June 8, Tuesday (evening)

We are twelve to thirteen days from Fort Laramie. Still thinking about how Mary might have saved me.

Day 31, June 9, Wednesday (evening)

Good campsite tonight, known as Ash Hollow to Fitzpatrick, abundance of wood available, pure water, plenty of grass for our animals. Not looking forward to tomorrow, going to be a hard day, I am being told.

Day 32, June 10, Thursday (morning)

Up early checking my wagon wheels and brakes. Emptied most of my water barrel to reduce weight.

Day 32, June 10 (evening)

Today, we descended the very steep Windlass Hill. Each wagon, one at a time, was let down by ropes. The slope seemed almost straight up and down. Only about three hundred feet from top to bottom but felt more like a mile. I had to keep my hand on the wheel brake during the descent the whole time while others controlled the ropes. After my wagon was down, I climbed back up the hill to help, until all wagons were down. Good news, all wagons down, no accidents. After our descent, we covered another ten miles.

Day 33, June 11, Friday (evening)

Today, we passed Courthouse Rock and its smaller companion, Jail Rock. These were the second landmarks on the trail. The larger rock is named for its similarity in appearance to the city of St. Louis courthouse, I am told. Some people have great imaginations but not me, apparently.

Day 34, June 12, Saturday (evening)

By midafternoon, we could begin to make out the spire of Chimney Rock. Tonight, we camped in an area with a large number of prairie dogs. We had seen the little animals before but never in such large numbers. There were hundreds of little heads popping up and down all over the place.

Day 35, June 13, Sunday (evening)

We reached Chimney Rock, maybe the most recognizable landmark on the trail. It looks like a large haystack with a pole in the middle. The flat prairie is changing, the trail is becoming steeper. The effect of the change is noticeable in both man and animal.

Day 36, June 14, Monday (morning)

Had a good night's sleep, ready to meet the day!

Day 37, June 15, Tuesday (evening)

Didn't travel as far today. We don't want to overwork our animals; some people very slow.

Day 38, June 16, Wednesday (evening)

This morning, as we readied to move on, Fitzpatrick called everyone together. He said, today we will pass by what is now known as Scotts Bluff. Like myself, Hiram Scott was a mountain man, trapper, and trader. In 1828, when he and two companions were returning to St. Louis from the 1828 rendezvous, he became ill. He continued for a few days with his companions until he could go no further. His two comrades placed him on a makeshift raft and attempted to transport him downstream. However, for some unknown reason, the two men abandoned Scott on the north bank of the Platte River. The next spring, Scott's skull was found on the other side of the river, below a set of bluffs, implying he had somehow managed to cross to the opposite bank before he died. The rest of his bones were found hundreds of yards from where he had been deserted. The bluff was named Scotts Bluff in his honor.

Day 39, June 17, Thursday (evening)

No sight of buffalo for two days.

Day 40, June 18, Friday (evening)

No sight of trees today. Land is flat but beautiful, as we travel through a flower-freckled prairie.

Day 41, June 19, Saturday (morning)

Had dinner with Sam and Mary. We talked more about our plans when we reach Oregon. I asked Sam if he would consider joining me and Daniel as a partner in our sawmill. I could see the surprise on both Sam and Mary's faces. They said they would think about it!

Day 42, June 20, Sunday (morning)

As the wagon train began moving, one of the party's small herd of milk cows bolted, spooked by something unseen moving through the grass. A group of men chased them down, but before the cows could be slowed down, one of them stepped into a gopher hole and broke its leg.

The rest of the party moved forward, as the owner of the cow and another wagon owner stayed behind to butcher the animal. They caught up with the wagon train several hours after we had made camp for the evening. Barbequed beef was on the menu for everyone!

Day 43, June 21, Monday (evening)

Out of coffee and sugar, should be able to resupply at Fort Laramie. Waiting to hear Sam and Mary's response.

Day 44, June 22, Tuesday (evening)

With a hard push today, we reached Fort Laramie by late afternoon. We plan to rest here at least one day. Provisions a dollar a pint for flour, a dollar a pound for coffee and sugar. Bought both coffee and sugar, three pairs of socks, and a pair of suspenders to keep my pants up! We have covered about a third of our journey. We are being told it is impossible to take our wagons through to Oregon: large parts of the trail are only walking trails, not wagon trails, and this is causing great concern. Mailed off the first part of my journal to Daniel and Whitney.

Day 45, June 23, Wednesday (morning)

Day off. Meeting was called to put an end to rumors we would not be able to get our wagons through to Oregon. Most people have settled down, I feel reassured. I was surprised to find there were several unattached men staying at the fort. One named Cochran has caught Betsey Gray's eye, and they went for a picnic.

> Originally established as a private fur trading fort in 1834, Fort Laramie evolved into the largest and best-known military post on the Northern Plains before its abandonment in 1890. This "grand old post" witnessed the entire sweeping saga of America's western expansion and Native American resistance to encroachment on their territories.

Day 46, June 24, Thursday (morning)

Morning off. Believe it or not, the word is, Betsey and Cochran are getting married today! I'm told Fort Laramie is a common place for weddings.

Day 47, June 25, Friday (morning)

Leaving Fort Laramie, headed to Fort Hall. Rested and resupplied. We are making our way west without Betsey!

Day 47, June 25 (evening)

Made good time today, covered at least twenty miles. Told we have hard days coming!

Day 48, June 26, Saturday (morning)

I had a dream last night, not the recurring dream but a new dream. I followed a small stream up into the hills. There were so many trees, I could not
walk in a straight line. Sam was walking with me.

Day 49, June 27, Sunday (evening)

Camped at Register Cliff. The chalky limestone bluff rises more than 100
feet above the North Platte River. According to Fitzpatrick, travelers often
carve their names and the date they stopped here, as a record for others
who follow. I found a clear space about four feet high and carved my name,
so it would be there for Daniel and Whitney to read.

Maybe it was loneliness, but I decided to get out the book Whitney got me
of *Grimms' Fairy Tales* and read it tonight. I chose the story of "The Golden
Bird."

THE GOLDEN BIRD

*A certain king had a beautiful garden, and in the garden stood a
tree which bore golden apples. These apples were always counted,
and about the time when they began to grow ripe it was found that
every night one of them was gone. The king became very angry at
this and ordered the gardener to keep watch all night under the tree.
The gardener set his eldest son to watch; but about twelve o'clock he
fell asleep, and in the morning another of the apples was missing.
Then the second son was ordered to watch; and at midnight he too
fell asleep, and in the morning another apple was gone. Then the
third son offered to keep watch; but the gardener at first would not
let him, for fear some harm should come to him: however, at last he
consented, and the young man laid himself under the tree to watch.
As the clock struck twelve, he heard a rustling noise in the air, and a
bird came flying that was of pure gold; and as it was snapping at one
of the apples with its beak, the gardener's son jumped up and shot an
arrow at it. But the arrow did the bird no harm; only it dropped a
golden feather from its tail, and then flew away. The golden feather
was brought to the king in the morning, and all the council was
called together. Everyone agreed that it was worth more than all the
wealth of the kingdom: but the king said, "One feather is of no use to
me, I must have the whole bird."*

Then the gardener's eldest son set out and thought to find the golden bird very easily; and when he had gone but a little way, he came to a wood, and by the side of the wood he saw a fox sitting; so he took his bow and made ready to shoot at it. Then the fox said, "Do not shoot me, for I will give you good counsel; I know what your business is, and that you want to find the golden bird. You will reach a village in the evening; and when you get there, you will see two inns opposite to each other, one of which is very pleasant and beautiful to look at: go not in there, but rest for the night in the other, though it may appear to you to be very poor and mean." But the son thought to himself, "What can such a beast as this know about the matter?" So he shot his arrow at the fox; but he missed it, and it set up its tail above its back and ran into the wood. Then he went his way, and in the evening came to the village where the two inns were; and in one of these were people singing, and dancing, and feasting; but the other looked very dirty, and poor. "I should be very silly," said he, "if I went to that shabby house, and left this charming place"; so he went into the smart house, and ate and drank at his ease, and forgot the bird, and his country too.

Time passed on; and as the eldest son did not come back, and no tidings were heard of him, the second son set out, and the same thing happened to him. He met the fox, who gave him the good advice: but when he came to the two inns, his eldest brother was standing at the window where the merrymaking was, and called to him to come in; and he could not withstand the temptation, but went in, and forgot the golden bird and his country in the same manner.

Time passed on again, and the youngest son too wished to set out into the wide world to seek for the golden bird; but his father would not listen to it for a long while, for he was very fond of his son, and was afraid that some ill luck might happen to him also, and prevent his coming back. However, at last it was agreed he should go, for he would not rest at home; and as he came to the wood, he met the fox, and heard the same good counsel. But he was thankful to the fox, and did not attempt his life as his brothers had done; so the fox said, "Sit upon my tail, and you will travel faster." So he sat down, and the fox began to run, and away they went over stock and stone so quick that their hair whistled in the wind.

When they came to the village, the son followed the fox's counsel, and without looking about him went to the shabby inn and rested there all night at his ease. In the morning came the fox again and met him as he was beginning his journey, and said, "Go straight forward, till you come to a castle, before which lie a whole troop of soldiers fast asleep and snoring: take no notice of them, but go into the castle and pass on and on till you come to a room, where the golden bird sits in a wooden cage; close by it stands a beautiful golden cage; but do not try to take the bird out of the shabby cage and put it into the handsome one, otherwise you will repent it." Then the fox stretched out his tail again, and the young man sat himself down, and away they went over stock and stone till their hair whistled in the wind.

Before the castle gate all was as the fox had said: so the son went in and found the chamber where the golden bird hung in a wooden cage, and below stood the golden cage, and the three golden apples that had been lost were lying close by it. Then thought he to himself, "It will be a very droll thing to bring away such a fine bird in this shabby cage'" so he opened the door and took hold of it and put it into the golden cage.

But the bird set up such a loud scream that all the soldiers awoke, and they took him prisoner and carried him before the king. The next morning the court sat to judge him; and when all was heard, it sentenced him to die, unless he should bring the king the golden horse which could run as swiftly as the wind; and if he did this, he was to have the golden bird given him for his own.

So he set out once more on his journey, sighing, and in great despair, when on a sudden his friend the fox met him, and said, "You see now what has happened on account of your not listening to my counsel. I will still, however, tell you how to find the golden horse, if you will do as I bid you. You must go straight on till you come to the castle where the horse stands in his stall: by his side will lie the groom fast asleep and snoring: take away the horse quietly, but be sure to put the old leathern saddle upon him, and not the golden one that is close by it."

Then the son sat down on the fox's tail, and away they went over stock and stone till their hair whistled in the wind. All went right, and the groom lay snoring with his hand upon the golden saddle. But when the son looked at the horse, he thought it a great pity to put the leathern saddle upon it. "I will give him the good one," said he; "I am sure he deserves it." As he took up the golden saddle the groom awoke and cried out so loud, that all the guards ran in and took him prisoner, and in the morning he was again brought before the court to be judged, and was sentenced to die. But it was agreed, that, if he *could bring thither the beautiful princess, he should live, and have the bird and the horse given him for his own.*

Then he went his way very sorrowful; but the old fox came and said, "Why did not you listen to me? If you had, you would have carried away both the bird and the horse; yet will I once more give you counsel. Go straight on, and in the evening you will arrive at a castle. At twelve o'clock at night the princess goes to the bathing-house: go up to her and give her a kiss, and she will let you lead her away; but take care you do not suffer her to go and take leave of her father and mother."

Then the fox stretched out his tail, and so away they went over stock and stone till their hair whistled again.

As they came to the castle, all was as the fox had said, and at twelve o'clock the young man met the princess going to the bath and gave her the kiss, and she agreed to run away with him, but begged with many tears that he would let her take leave of her father. At first he refused, but she wept still more and more, and fell at his feet, till at last he consented; but the moment she came to her father's house the guards awoke and he was taken prisoner again.

Then he was brought before the king, and the king said, "You shall never have my daughter unless in eight days you dig away the hill that stops the view from my window." Now this hill was so big that the whole world could not take it away: and when he had worked for seven days, and had done very little, the fox came and said. "Lie down and go to sleep; I will work for you." And in the morning he awoke and the hill was gone; so he went merrily to the king, and told him that now that it was removed he must give him the princess.

Then the king was obliged to keep his word, and away went the young man and the princess; and the fox came and said to him, "We will have all three, the princess, the horse, and the bird." "Ah!" said the young man, "that would be a great thing, but how can you contrive it?"

"If you will only listen," said the fox, "it can be done. When you come to the king, and he asks for the beautiful princess, you must say, 'Here she is!' Then he will be very joyful; and you will mount the golden horse that they are to give you, and put out your hand to take leave of them; but shake hands with the princess last. Then lift her

quickly on to the horse behind you; clap your spurs to his side, and gallop away as fast as you can."

All went right: then the fox said, "When you come to the castle where the bird is, I will stay with the princess at the door, and you will ride in and speak to the king; and when he sees that it is the right horse, he will bring out the bird; but you must sit still, and say that you want to look at it, to see whether it is the true golden bird; and when you get it into your hand ride away."

This, too, happened as the fox said; they carried off the bird, the princess mounted again, and they rode on to a great wood. Then the fox came, and said, "Pray kill me, and cut off my head and my feet." But the young man refused to do it: so the fox said, "I will at any rate give you good counsel: beware of two things; ransom no one from the gallows, and sit down by the side of no river." Then away he went. "Well," thought the young man, "it is no hard matter to keep that advice."

He rode on with the princess, till at last he came to the village where he had left his two brothers. And there he heard a great noise and uproar; and when he asked what the matter was, the people said, "Two men are going to be hanged." As he came nearer, he saw that the two men were his brothers, who had turned robbers; so he said, "Cannot they in any way be saved?" But the people said "No," unless he would bestow all his money upon the rascals and buy their liberty. Then he did not stay to think about the matter, but paid what was asked, and his brothers were given up, and went on with him towards their home.

And as they came to the wood where the fox first met them, it was so cool and pleasant that the two brothers said, "Let us sit down by the side of the river, and rest a while, to eat and drink." So he said, "Yes," and forgot the fox's counsel, and sat down on the side of the river; and while he suspected nothing, they came behind, and threw him down the bank, and took the princess, the horse, and the bird, and went home to the king their master, and said. "All this have we won by our labor." Then there was great rejoicing made; but the horse would not eat, the bird would not sing, and the princess wept.

The youngest son fell to the bottom of the river's bed: luckily it was nearly dry, but his bones were almost broken, and the bank was so steep that he could find no way to get out. Then the old fox came *once more, and scolded him for not following his advice; otherwise no evil would have befallen him: "Yet," said he, "I cannot leave you here, so lay hold of my tail and hold fast." Then he pulled him out of the river, and said to him, as he got upon the bank, "Your brothers have set watch to kill you, if they find you in the kingdom." So he dressed himself as a poor man, and came secretly to the king's court, and was scarcely within the doors when the horse began to eat, and the bird to sing, and the princess left off weeping. Then he went to the king, and told him all his brothers' roguery; and they were seized and punished, and he had the princess given to him again; and after the king's death he was heir to his kingdom.*

A long while after, he went to walk one day in the wood, and the old fox met him, and besought him with tears in his eyes to kill him, and cut off his head and feet. And at last he did so, and in a moment the fox was changed into a man, and turned out to be the brother of the princess, who had been lost a great many, many, years.

Day 50, June 28, Monday (evening)

Traveled today, no rest, put nineteen to twenty miles behind us.

Day 51, June 29, Tuesday (evening)

Today, we climbed a hill with huge, deep ruts caused by weathering, very hard on animals and wagons. Five wagons got stuck badly. We needed extra animals to pull and many hands to push to get them out. Made less than ten miles today.

Day 52, June 30, Wednesday (evening)

Hot summer day, thunderstorm began brewing by midmorning. We had to stop, as a strong windstorm came up suddenly. After the storm passed, we traveled until we reached where we needed to cross the river. The river is about one hundred feet wide, and the water is clear but very swift.

After a quick meeting, it was decided it was too dangerous to try to ford the river. Instead, we would need to build two rafts and ferry our wagons across. A half-dozen men, one of which was I, were given the task to chop down several cottonwood trees. This was my time to shine. I had practiced my axe skills diligently before we left. After the trees were down, others were given the responsibility to build the rafts. By evening, the rafts had been built.

Day 53, July 1, Thursday (evening)

Up before daylight. Half the animals were led across the river along with several ropes. The rafts were put in place, the first wagons loaded aboard, the wheels were then removed and the wagon lowered; it was now ready to be hauled across the river by pole and ropes. Having reached the other side, the wagon's wheels were reattached and the wagon removed from the raft. The raft was then sent back across by rope to start its journey again. By the end of the day, more than half the wagons were on the other side.

Day 54, July 2, Friday (evening)

Up before daylight again. By afternoon, all wagons were on the west side of the river and ready for travel.

Day 55, July 3, Saturday (evening)

We arrived in the late afternoon at Independence Rock. There is an abundance of grass. Our goal was to make it here before July 4, which we have.

Day 56, July 4, Sunday (evening)

A day of hard-earned rest. I took my fiddle out and entertained myself.

Day 57, July 5, Monday (evening)

Today we played a new game called Rounders. You pound in four stakes in a square pattern roughly thirty paces apart. Other items needed include a cloth ball (made from canvas) and a large rolling pin. Teams consist of between nine and fifteen players. One team spreads out amongst the stakes, known as the field. The team in the field has a designated player, called the pitcher, who tosses the ball to the first member of the other team, who is known as the batter. The batter stands at skate number one with the rolling-pin. When the pitcher tosses the ball, the batter tries to hit the ball. If the batter misses the ball, he gets one more try; if he hits the ball, he runs to stake number two. He must get there before the team in the field touches the stake with the ball. Then the next batter takes his turn. If he hits the ball, he runs to stake number two, while the player at stake two must advance to stake number three. If the team in the field touches either stake two or three before the runner arrives, that player is out. The team up to bat continues, trying to advance their players from stake to stake. If a player makes it all the way around the square and back to stake number one, he scores a run. After all team members have a turn, the teams switch places. Each team gets three turns, then the game is over.

Day 58, July 6, Tuesday (evening)

By midmorning, we came in sight of Devil's Gate. When we halted for lunch, many of us paid a visit to the gate. It is indeed a sight worth seeing. The river has carved a channel through what appears to be solid rock. The gate's cliffs are several hundred feet high on each side and nearly perpendicular.

Day 59, July 7, Wednesday (morning)

Rested and excited. Each step is a step closer to Oregon.

Day 60, July 8, Thursday (evening)

Invited Sam and Mary to dinner (made pancakes), asked if they had considered my offer. They said they want to be partners!

Day 61, July 9, Friday (evening)

During our travel today, one of the wagons wheels came off. The wagon train halted for about an hour while it was fixed. Everyone else was told to check their wagons. I took the opportunity to grease my wagon wheels and check the metal rims. When we stopped for the day, I soaked my wheels and tarred my wagon.

Day 62, July 10, Saturday (evening)

Now heading northwest. The trail is sandy. Crossed Sweetwater River several times today. River is shallow and easily navigated.

Day 63, July 11, Sunday (morning)

Trial of Mr. Moss for falling asleep while standing guard, sentenced to five lashes. Did not watch, but others did. More river crossings today.

Day 64, July 12, Monday (evening)

Camped at Ice Slough, an amazing place! Fitzpatrick has been telling us stories about this place for a couple days, but I didn't believe him. He said, if we dig a little below the surface in this low, swampy place, we would find ice. When we arrived, he took us there. We dug down about twelve inches, and, sure enough, we found pure ice, ten inches thick! We broke-up the ice and carried chunks back to our water barrels.

Day 65, July 13, Tuesday (evening)

More river crossings today. Water in my barrel still cold.

Day 66, July 14, Wednesday (morning)

Since Sam and I are now partners, we are starting to make plans. I suggested once we get to Oregon, we should visit the Hudson's Bay Company at Fort Vancouver to get information about where to settle. He said, do you think they will help us, since we are Americans and they are a British company? I said, even the British need lumber!

> *Fort Vancouver was a trading post located on the northern bank of the Columbia River in present-day Vancouver, Washington. Furs from Fort Vancouver were shipped to China and exchanged for goods to be sold in the United Kingdom.*

Day 67, July 15, Thursday (evening)

It is clear we are climbing in elevation; I can feel it in my legs, and I can see it in the horizon. Word is we will reach South Pass soon.

Day 68, July 16, Friday (morning)

Reached South Pass. Halfway point, we are on the Continental Divide. Had problems staking down the horses, as the ground is very rocky.

> *South Pass (elevation 7,412 feet and 7,550 feet) is the collective term for two mountain passes on the Continental Divide, in the Rocky Mountains in southwestern Wyoming. South Pass is the lowest point on the Continental Divide between the Central and Southern Rocky Mountains. The passes furnish a natural crossing point of the Rockies. The historic pass became the route for emigrants on the Oregon, California, and Mormon trails to the West during the nineteenth century.*

Day 69, July 17, Saturday (evening)

Stopped at a marshy area known as Pacific Springs, filled up our water barrels. Springs are named Pacific, because now all streams are flowing west to the Pacific Ocean.

Day 70, July 18, Sunday (morning)

Day off, spent time with Sam and Mary. Father De Smet will be leaving us soon. Today, he spoke briefly. Afterwards, someone asked if she could share how she came to place her faith in Jesus. Several others followed. I wasn't sure I wanted to share—I'm not the greatest speaker—but there was a lull, so I decided to tell my story.

"My father owned a sawmill, and sometimes I rode along with him on his delivery trips to Independence and we'd talk. He'd tell me stories from the Bible, and I'd listen intently. He always said, there are five important things to having a good life. If you always work hard and are honest, people will respect you; the closest thing to heaven you will experience here on earth is the love of your family, so love your wife like she's the most precious thing on this earth and raise your children to be God-fearing, and they will be a joy and not a burden. Be resolute and never be afraid to dream; but, above all, love God with all your heart.

"I remember asking him, how do you love God with all your heart?

"He said, 'First, you have to ask God into your heart, and you do that by placing your faith in God's Son, Jesus. The Bible says in John 3:16, "For God so loved the world, that he gave his only begotten Son, that whosoever believeth in him should not perish, but have everlasting life."'"

"So, I bowed my head and repeated John 3:16 and asked Jesus into my heart."

A few others went after me, including Mary. It was a great day!

Day 71, July 19, Monday (morning)

The grasslands of the Plains have now been replaced by scrub brush and sagebrush. The soil is much drier and sandy.

Day 72, July 20, Tuesday (morning)

On our way again, next stop will be Fort Hall.

Day 73, July 21, Wednesday (evening)

Wagon problems today, not mine, but others, and we are still several days from any kind of supplies. A few people have an extra wheel; one was used today.

Day 74, July 22, Thursday (morning)

Coyotes howling all night long, hard to sleep! Meeting with Sam and Mary tonight.

Day 75, July 23, Friday (morning)

Explained to Sam, the most important decision we will make is location. We must find a place suitable to build our mill. We need a year-round stream strong enough to turn the waterwheel with sufficient speed! After that, it would be nice to have some flat land for field animals and, more importantly, tons and tons of trees. Big, tall, straight, evergreen fir trees

Day 76, July 24, Saturday (evening)

More coyotes howling last night. A few gun shots as well. I don't think they hit anything, but the howling stopped!

Day 77, July 25, Sunday (evening)

Crossed a small stream that meanders across the plateau several times today.

Day 78, July 26, Monday (evening)

We saw evidence of Indians today. Fitzpatrick says there is nothing to worry about, they are just curious!

Day 79, July 27, Tuesday (evening)

Long day, tired, going to sleep early before the sun goes down and the night sounds start again.

Day 80, July 28, Wednesday (morning)

Slept well! Got up early and greased my wagon. Put grease on my lips as well. Water barrel is low, will need to fill it up soon.

Day 81, July 29, Thursday (evening)

The Indians we spotted a few days ago made contact this afternoon. They arrived to escort Father De Smet to the Flathead tribes. Stopped by a small stream and filled my water barrel. The Indians shared some food with us they called pemmican.

The term Flathead was the nickname given by Europeans to any Native Americans who intentionally changed the shape of their heads to a flat, elongated profile. These tribes included the Coast Salish, the Chinooks, the Clatsop, Cowlitz, and the Wahkiakum tribes.

Pemmican is a mixture of tallow, dried meat, and dried berries, used as a nutritious food. Historically, it was an important part of indigenous cuisine in certain parts of North America and is still prepared today.

Day 82, July 30, Friday (morning)

Father De Smet leaving to travel to the Flathead Indians. Said my farewell, I'm going to miss him!

Day 82, July 30 (evening)

Arrived at Soda Springs. Our group will split tomorrow. The group going to California is headed by Mr. Bidwell, so we said our goodbyes tonight.

> *Natural bubbling pools of carbonated water, caused by ancient volcanic activity, have long made Soda Springs an attraction. Local Native Americans, fur traders, and trappers visited the springs prior to the days of the Oregon Trail emigrations. Emigrants used the pools of water for medicinal and bathing purposes. Many pioneers and their animals became sick when they drank too much of the alkali water from the springs.*

Day 83, July 31, Saturday (morning)

Both groups are packed and ready to leave. We leave first. Our next stop is Fort Hall.

Day 84, Aug. 1, Sunday (evening)

Stopped by Steamboat Springs. This geyser spews carbonated water periodically in geyser-like fashion, making loud chugging noises like a steamboat.

Day 85, Aug. 2, Monday (evening)

Rainy morning cold and unpleasant, late start. Rained all day, but has now stopped.

Day 86, Aug. 3, Tuesday (evening)

Should reach Fort Hall tomorrow, need a few supplies.

Day 87, Aug. 4, Wednesday (morning) - Fort Hall

Reached Fort Hall. I was able to buy all needed supplies, including grain feed for my horses. Prices are fair, the best place to get supplies yet! We plan to remain at Fort Hall for three days. Mailed the second part of my journal back to Daniel and Whitney.

> *Fort Hall was a fur trading post located on the Snake River in eastern Oregon, which is now in southeastern Idaho.*

Day 88, Aug. 5, Thursday (evening)—Fort Hall

Took a walk with Sam and Mary this morning, then we had dinner together.

Day 89, Aug. 6, Friday (evening)—Fort Hall

We had a group picnic, with most of the supplies provided by those living at the fort, who joined us for food and games. We played rounders and horse shoes. Played my fiddle along with others. This is where I said my goodbye to Mr. Fitzpatrick, an amazing man, and I can say a true friend. He had finished his job. Father DeSmet was on his way to the Flathead Indian tribes, escorted by the Indians themselves. We would now be led by an employee from Fort Hall to the Whitman Mission, while Broken Hand would be returning to Independence.

Day 90, Aug. 7, Saturday (evening) - Fort Hall

Day of rest, not really, just no travel, spent all day caring for my horses, brushed them out and cared for their feet, gave them an extra amount of food. Checked my wagon, repacked some items; sadly, a few of the glass panes are cracked. Leaving tomorrow morning for Whitman Mission

Day 91, Aug. 8, Sunday (evening)

More sagebrush than anything else today, but I did actually see a coyote it ran right across my path, first time I have actually seen one close-up. It looked like a skinny, light brown/gray-haired dog.

Day 92, Aug. 9, Monday (evening)

Today, we started following the Snake River. This evening, I took my fiddle out and played it for about an hour. The stars are bright, and the sky is like a deep blue sea.

Day 93, Aug. 10, Tuesday (morning)

Had coffee with Sam and Mary before we pulled out for the day. Sam said Mary has morning sickness, whatever that is?

Day 94, Aug. 11, Wednesday (evening)

Found out what morning sickness is! Days are long, nights much warmer. We seem to be meandering toward the horizon each day, but we never get there. The river is bending and turning all the time like a snake.

> *At the time, the Snake River was called the Lewis Fork of the Columbia River (named after Meriwether Lewis).*

Day 95, Aug. 12, Thursday (evening)

Traveled fifteen miles today, had to stop for an hour, small accident, child fell off horse—probably fell asleep, not a serious injury. We are still following the river, but the river is in a canyon as much as two hundred feet below us, and we are on a flat plain above it. The canyon walls are black, and I'm told the black rock is lava.

Day 96, Aug. 13, Friday (evening)

The ground is very dry and soft, animals are having to work harder pulling our wagons.

Day 97, Aug. 14, Saturday (evening)

Pleasant day, soft breeze, air somewhat smoky, reminds me of an autumn day at home. We arrived at what is called Three Island Crossing, stopped for the evening. Our guide told us the water level is low enough that our crossing should be safe but time-consuming.

Day 98, Aug. 15, Sunday (evening)

We started crossing the Lewis River today at Three Island Crossing. We tied four wagons together, with two handlers for each animal team and a rope. The first group which included me, crossed the river where it was about a hundred yards wide to the first island. The river depth reached the bottom of the wagons at places. The rope was then tied off to a wagon on each side of the first section of the river, and all women and children crossed safely to the first island. After a few minutes rest, a second rope was strung across to the second island, about seventy yards further. The water was not as high but swifter. After a few minutes, three wagons crossed the last section of the river easily. This section of the river was very shallow with little current. The fourth wagon was used to tie off the rope between first and second island. Next, all women and children were escorted to the far side of the river, using the ropes as security. With all women and children across, all remaining animals not needed for wagons were driven across. In two chains, all remaining wagons crossed last. It was late afternoon by the time everything and everyone had made it safely across. It was decided to camp near the river for the night.

> *Three Island Crossing was the most important and difficult river crossing on the Snake River. It is located near what is today Glenns Ferry, Idaho. Pioneers forded the Snake River at the Three Island Crossing until 1869, when Gustavus "Gus" Glenn constructed a ferry about two miles upstream, primarily to expedite freight but also for emigrants. His boat, which could hold two wagons, cut nearly twenty miles from the former route.*

Day 99, Aug. 16, Monday (morning)

Didn't cool off much last night, hard to sleep. Already very warm this morning. Told we have about a day and a half until we reach Salmon Falls, and about eighteen to twenty days until we reach Farewell Bend, where we stop following the river and head up over the Blue Mountains to the Whitman Mission.

Day 100, Aug. 17, Tuesday (evening)

We got up and left two hours early, took a midafternoon break to stay out of the hot sun, then traveled into the early evening before stopping. We reached Salmon Falls today.

> Salmon Falls was a series of falls on the Snake River. The falls have now been cut off by the Lower Salmon Falls Dam Reservoir.

Day 101, Aug. 18, Wednesday (morning)

Weather changed during the night, woke up to an overcast sky. Made breakfast and lunch, then greased my wagon wheels before we left. Gave my horses extra grain.

Day 101, Aug. 18 (evening)

One hundred days since we left Independence. In some ways, it seems just like yesterday; in others, it seems like years. Once I started thinking about it, I became a little homesick, lonely.

Day 102, Aug. 19, Thursday (evening)

We stopped by a small stream. Everyone filled their water barrels and watered their animals before bathing their bodies.

Day 103, Aug. 20, Friday (morning)

I cooked dinner for Sam and Mary this evening. Warm night.

Day 104, Aug. 21, Saturday (evening)

Our path today was strewn with large boulders and a ground cover called knotted sage.

Day 105, Aug. 22, Sunday (morning)

Last night, one of our party shot a rattlesnake, then cut the rattler off. We seem to be in the area of a large population of long-eared rabbits.

The jackrabbit's long ears reminded some people of a donkey's ears. Sometimes, the jackrabbit was referred to as a jackass rabbit.

Day 106, Aug. 23, Monday (evening)

Very hot all day long. We crossed a tributary of the Lewis River before noon. Stopped to water animals. I dipped myself in the river. While it was little harder walking soaking wet, it felt good.

Day 107, Aug. 24, Tuesday (morning)

Can't be too far now before we turn north and head over the mountains. Their height stands out in stark contrast to the flat prairie we are crossing.

Day 108, Aug. 25, Wednesday (evening)

Heat is exhausting. When we stopped for the day, I turned my wagon to the sun and used it to create shade for myself and my horses. Made sure horses had plenty of water. Didn't eat until it was dark.

Day 109, Aug. 26, Thursday (evening)

Today, we reached Farewell Bend. Tomorrow, we will start over the Blue Mountains to the Whitman Mission.

After following the Snake River for 330 miles, Oregon Trail pioneers rested above the bend in the river here, then bid farewell to the Snake River and continued their trek.

The Blue Mountains are a mountain range in the western United States, located largely in northeastern Oregon and stretching into southeastern Washington. The Blue Mountains were so named due to the color of the mountains when seen from a distance. In the 1800s, the Blue Mountains were a formidable obstacle to settlers traveling on the Oregon Trail and were often the last mountain range American pioneers had to cross before either reaching southeast Washington near Walla Walla or passing down the Columbia River Gorge to the end of the Oregon Trail in the Willamette Valley near Oregon City.

Day 110, Aug. 27, Friday (evening)

Our guide explained to us before we started this morning the importance of keeping our wagons moving straight up and down the slopes to avoid tipping over on the sidehills. We traveled only nine to ten miles today. We had to harness extra teams to each wagon twice to climb the hills. We are now in the trees, and this evening the air is alive with birds. It is my first glimpse of the kind of trees described by Mr. Lee, and they are beautiful!

Day 111, Aug. 28, Saturday (evening)

Today was the toughest day yet since leaving Independence. We are now either cutting a path through the trees or removing fallen trees from our path. The good news: it's not hot here, like down below, and our guide says in another day we will be out of the trees and into the alpine meadows of the mountains. I did not see them, but others reported seeing a moose and several elk. I'm so tired, I will sleep well tonight!

Day 112, Aug. 29, Sunday (evening)

The best way to describe our journey today would be: climb one hill, descend a hill, climb another hill. Tonight, we are camped at one of the most beautiful places I have ever seen; there are wildflowers and sage everywhere! We are camped at a clear, cool mountain lake. Tomorrow, we start our descent. But tonight, there are more butterflies than I can count and the sound of birds singing!

Day 113, Aug. 30, Monday (evening)

Our Indian guide tells us we will reach Whitman Mission tomorrow. Our descent was easier than the climb. I saw an elk for the first time, and there is an abundance of deer here as well. By midafternoon, we could see flat land again.

Day 114, Aug. 31, Tuesday (morning)

Reached Whitman Mission. At the mission, we purchased wheat and ground it on a hand mill, had pickled pork and fresh tomatoes. The Indians are very civilized. They said prayers in the evening and sang Christian songs.

Day 115, Sept. 1, Wednesday (morning)—Whitman Mission

A day of rest! Spent time with Sam and Mary.

Day 116, Sept. 2, Thursday (evening)—Whitman Mission

Day of rest. Dr. Whitman has a very comfortable house and well-cultivated fields. The mission has a threshing machine and a grinding mill powered by water. They sold us provisions at reasonable prices compared to the other forts at which we had stopped.

Day 117, Sept. 3, Friday (evening)—Whitman Mission

Day of rest. I had a long visit with the guide who had led us from Fort Hall to the Whitman Mission. I asked him if he had been from here to Fort Vancouver. He said he had many times. He gave me several concerns, and the largest is the last leg of our journey!

Day 118, Sept. 4, Saturday (evening)

Up early before the sun came up. We are starting for The Dalles (they say it like *dalz*) this morning, and Doctor Whitman has sent an Indian guide with us. We covered at least fifteen miles before noon, traveled until midafternoon, stopped to get out of the midday heat. After the sun set, we traveled another two hours before making camp for the night.

Day 119, Sept. 5, Sunday (evening)

Early start again. We repeated the same schedule as yesterday. The trail is flat to rolling hills. We can see ahead for miles, so I tried to pick out a landmark and keep my eye on it to judge our progress.

Day 120, Sept. 6, Monday (evening)

Woke up to an overcast sky. Our guide says it should be good for travel. I am getting anxious, like when you're a child and your birthday is just a few days away. Tonight, I spoke with Sam and Mary about what the guide had told me about the last leg of our journey from The Dalles to Fort Vancouver. He said we would have to float our wagons on rafts down the Columbia River; there is no trail between.

Day 121, Sept. 7, Tuesday (morning)

Early start. Sky is clear, and it's going to be hot. The plan is to take a midday rest and then travel into the evening again. There are no trees in sight. The sky remains semi-light all night.

Day 122, Sept. 8, Wednesday (evening)

The country over which we are traveling is mostly covered with bunch grass, of which animals are fond. We could see tops of mountains in the distance for the first time. They struck fear in many of us, as their lofty peaks seemed the resting place of the clouds. Sam, Mary, and I continued our previous conversation. The guide suggested we sell our animals in The Dalles and buy new animals when we reached Fort Vancouver. I told them I couldn't do that; my horses are special, and we need them to log with. The guide said there is a walking trail but not a wagon trail. I said I want you to float our wagons down the river, and I will walk the horses by foot. The guide said you just follow the river; you can't miss the fort.

Day 123, Sept. 9, Thursday (evening)

We are now following the Columbia River. The river has carved out a large gorge. Today, we traveled across a plateau high above the river, and there was a wind blowing in our face most of the day!

Day 124, Sept. 10, Friday (evening)

Our guide says we will reach The Dalles tomorrow. Covered lots of grassland today, as we continue to follow the river. This evening we finalized our plans. Sam and Mary will sell their animals at The Dalles and bring our wagons by raft; I will walk my horses to Fort Vancouver.

Day 125, Sept. 11 and 12, Saturday / Sunday

Reached The Dalles. A very bustling town. After setting up our camp, several of us went into town to buy supplies and to find out whom we should contact about floating our wagons to Fort Vancouver. Had dinner at a hotel. They asked if I wanted a beer. I said no.

We hired Indian guides to float our wagons, but we will have to wait four days for our turn. Last night, I had the dream again, but this time I could see the woman's face: it was Mary! I have no idea why she is in my dreams!

Day 126, Sept. 13, Monday (evening)

Sam and I talked. Since we have to wait several days for guides to raft our wagons down the river, why don't we change plans; instead of them waiting for me, I will meet them at Fort Vancouver.

Day 127, Sept. 14, Tuesday (morning)

After talking with Sam and Mary again, I made plans to leave tomorrow morning, and I will meet them when they get there.

Day 128, Sept. 15, Wednesday (evening)

Said my goodbyes, then my horses and I crossed the river and started west. The trail is not very wide but passable. Stopped in the late afternoon, made a fire, cooked some food, then went swimming in the Columbia. It was cool but felt good! The stars are out tonight, and I'm a little bit lonely.

Day 129, Sept. 16, Thursday (morning)

Sam and Mary should begin their trip down the Columbia River by raft today.

Day 129, Sept. 16 (evening)

Today, I saw rafts with wagons on them floating down the river. I waved at them and they waved back! Stopped a couple of times to let the horses rest and drink. I thought to myself, they must think this is a piece of cake, compared to pulling the wagon. Took some time to skip rocks in the river this evening. I haven't done that for a long time.

Day 130, Sept. 17, Friday (morning)

Should reach the fort sometime today. Not sure what to do then, but I guess I'll figure it out when I get there.

Day 130, Sept. 17 (evening)

Reached the fort this afternoon, introduced myself. They said I was welcome to camp at the fort and that the Indians at the fort were locals. I'm hoping Sam and Mary will arrive tomorrow.

Day 131, Sept. 18, Saturday (evening)

Sam and Mary arrived before noon. The wheels were put back on the wagons, then the wagons were brought ashore with the horses. Pulled our wagons to where I'd made camp and we celebrated; we have made it to Oregon!

Day 132, Sept. 19, Sunday (morning)

It feels like the first day of the future! It's now time to start putting the pieces of my dreams together. Today, I'm meeting with Dr. McLoughlin, chief factor of Fort Vancouver.

Day 132, Sept. 19 (evening)

Dr. McLoughlin is a very cordial man. We discussed our plans to build a sawmill. He was very encouraging, sent me to meet with John, the fort carpenter. After our meetings, we bought some fresh potatoes, carrots, and elk meat from the fort store. Mary made a tasty stew!

Day 133, Sept. 20, Monday (morning)

I looked back upon the precarious trail I had traveled with a degree of romance and pleasure, knowing that, to others, it was a graveyard of family and friends. The last thing I have to do is mail the last part of my journal back to Daniel and Whitney.

Day 134, Sept. 21, Tuesday (evening)

We are being encouraged by Dr. McLoughlin to join the other Americans and settle across the river in the Willamette Valley; but after meeting with John the fort carpenter, we might stay on the north side of the river. He has told us about a place he thinks will suit our needs well.

Day 135, Sept. 22, Wednesday (morning)

Daniel, this is the last part of my journal. I hope everything is going well for you and Whitney, hope to see you soon!

CHAPTER 3

<hr>

Second Interview

AFTER READING THOMAS'S CHRONICLE, I scheduled a time we could meet and I could return his journal. I told him I also had a number of questions for him. He said he would try to do his best to answer them. What follows is our conversation.

Thomas, after reading your journal, I was impressed, but it left me with questions I wanted to know the answers to, so I hope you don't mind if I ask you a few questions.

The first question is about the dream.[1] Did you have other dreams along the way or just this one?

I had other dreams, but none were as vivid or real to me. I guess that's why I recorded it in my journal.

Had you had other dreams or premonitions like this, growing up?

No, none before and none since, except maybe about the fire.

After having the dreams, did your relationship change with Sam and Mary?

<hr>

1. Day 7, May 16, Sunday (morning) Very quiet morning, everyone keeping to themselves. There were definitely several people very upset about the loss of their animals. Last night, I had a very vivid dream. I saw myself walking along a clear, flowing river on a narrow trail, under towering trees that seemed to touch the sky like mountains. Next, I was standing in an open field and walking towards a log house. I could see a young woman and two children standing outside, and then I woke up.
Day 24, June 2, Wednesday (morning) I had the dream again. I was walking towards a log house, I could see a young woman, and this time I recognized her.

No. Maybe.

What does maybe mean?

I definitely thought Mary was pretty!

Wait! Are you saying you had a dream about the Yacolt Burn?

It's odd, but about a week before the fire, I dreamed the same dream three nights in a row.

What was the dream?

I was in a wagon and I was fleeing a fire, then I'd wake-up!

Interesting. Let's talk about some other things, what was the hardest thing you had to deal with, on the journey west?

I don't know if there was one particular thing that was the hardest. Instead, there were several things, and the first was homesickness. Leaving everything and everyone you know is hard. The first few weeks I cried every night. I think that's why Sam and Mary's friendship became so important to me. Probably the next thing was the constant walking—not because I wasn't in shape. It was just monotonous, day after day. There were days it was hard to tell you had traveled. Everything looked the same as it did when you started the day. Lastly, I would have to say, when doubt crept into my mind.

What do you mean by doubt?

Maybe not so much doubt, but fear of the unknown.

You sent your brother your journals. Did you give him any other advice?

No, I hoped the journal would be helpful. But I tried not to show fear or doubt, because I didn't to want to scare him from coming!

Tell me about Father De Smet.

It was a joy to make his acquaintance. He was easy to talk to. More than once, we shared a water hole for a bath. He had a true heart for the conversion of the Indians. Besides his sermons, he had so many great stories to tell.

Others discarded items along the trail, because they overpacked and took un-needed items. Did you discard anything?

No, others brought too much, and it overworked their animals and they had to discard items to lighten the load. I had a very heavy wagon—much of it had to do with my sawmill—but I had six strong horses, and when I could, I used only four horses and gave the other two a break.

You wrote your name on Register Cliff. Did your brother find it?

He did, and both Daniel and Whitney signed their names next to mine.

What was your favorite part of the journey?

In many respects, I enjoyed the majority of the journey from a landscape perspective. I loved Courthouse Rock, Chimney Rock, Independence Rock, Ice Slough, Soda Springs, the Blue Mountains, and the last leg following the Columbia River.

What was the worst part of the trip, other than walking?

The early part of the trip, when I couldn't get to sleep because of the dogs barking and other animals howling. But eventually I began to just block out the noise and learned to go to sleep.

Tell me about the lashing of Mr. Moss.

I understood why, but I didn't agree with it. I stood there, but I couldn't watch. I just closed my eyes and thought about something else.

What was your favorite place?

I would say Fort Hall. It was a place of saying goodbyes, and plans were cemented for the future.

What did you think about the Indians you met?

It's hard to judge others you don't really know. I had some fear when they followed us, but I was impressed by those who came to take Father De Smet to their people, and those we met at the Whitman Mission.

You obviously wrote a great deal about the Sunday sermons in your journal. Why?

I think it was my way of confirming my faith in God and His Son, Jesus Christ. Writing about the sermons only helped me confirm my faith, and this journey was a leap of faith!

How did the trip change you?

The trip changed my life in many ways. It gave me confidence I could accomplish anything I put my mind and heart to, and it brought people into my life that would change my life!

Last question: what would you title the next chapter in this story?

"Expect the Unexpected."

What do you mean?

Things have a way of changing, and they don't always go as you've planned, and things aren't always what you assume.

Tell me about it!

CHAPTER 4

<hr>

Expect the Unexpected

WHEN WE FINALLY REACHED Fort Vancouver, I was relieved. I felt like we had survived the arduous journey unscathed, for the most part, and we could now actually begin making plans in earnest. I expected a collection of half-crazed fur trappers living in hovels; but, instead, I found the fort to be a spacious setting with elegantly built homes with the finest comforts. Our host, Dr. McLoughlin, was not a tyrant but a gracious host who invited us to dine with him. We found ourselves sitting down to an elegant dinner, served on fine china. Definitely not what I expected.

He welcomed us like long-lost friends and took a real interest in our future plans. He suggested we settle south of the Columbia River, noting we would find a growing community of fellow Americans in the Willamette Valley. He invited us to spend a few days at the fort and explained we could purchase needed supplies from the company store, which included animals, tack, utensils, seeds, and fresh fruits and vegetables.

The next morning, I visited every station at the fort—the blacksmith, the barns—but what caught my attention the most was the shipyard. I watched as a middle-aged man replaced several planks of wood on a docked sailing ship. I approached him, introduced myself, and explained my plans to build a sawmill; could he use such supplies? His face lit up, and we struck up a robust conversation. I explained I had carried the parts to a water-driven sawmill from Missouri and planned to produce milled lumber, and I desired to find a piece of property with both timber and a sufficient stream to power my sawmill.

He looked me over, then smiled at me and said, "I not only know of the perfect location, I'm sure the fort would be more than happy to purchase the majority of your finished product. At this time, we bring all our milled wood in by ship."

He introduced himself as John and explained he was a shipbuilder by trade. The Hudson Bay Fur Company had brought him to the Oregon Country from England a decade ago to repair their ships when needed. "When there is work, they send word to me and I come into the fort, where I stay until the job is finished." He continued, "There is a nice plot of land just to the west of my place with a year-round stream that flows out of the hills with sufficient force to turn a waterwheel, and the property is covered with a vast supply of trees."

I asked if there was enough land for two families.

He said, "Where I live, there are no neighbors for miles in either direction, and I've got all the land I need."

I asked, "Is it in the Willamette Valley?"

"No, it's on the north side of the river about twenty miles from here, up the Lewis River, a good-sized tributary of the Columbia River. There's a small community at the mouth of the river, but I live about four miles upriver."

"I thought Dr. McLoughlin said most of the Americans were south of the Columbia River?"

"Oh, they are, and the truth is, he wants to keep them there, but there are a few Americans who live north of the river, as well as some Brits like myself. The property I'm thinking of borders the river, and it has a large flat field that's perfect for a farm and a sawmill."

When our conversation was over, I went to find Sam to tell him what I'd learned. Together, we returned to speak to John some more. Last night, we were all set to go south of the river, but after this unexpected encounter with John, I had changed my mind. I now believed we should take a few days and go scout this property. The success of our future plans and lives were all dependent on finding the ideal piece of land. The wheels in my mind were really turning now: a year-round stream to power the sawmill and an abundance of tall straight trees ready to turn into lumber—all I had been dreaming of for the last two years. Ever since I began making my way west from The Dalles, my excitement had been growing as I passed through the forests of large Douglas fir trees that seemed to be everywhere. They are just as Mr. Lee had described them when I heard him speak, going on four years ago. Their magnificence had only confirmed my decision to undertake this journey halfway across the continent.

Now with the crucial decision on where to settle looming, I somehow knew we were meant to be north of the Columbia River—not south of the river— and it was all because of this chance meeting with John.

Sam and I set out early the next morning on horseback with a crude drawn map provided to us by John. From the fort, it was an easy trail north. The trail followed the riverbank and, for the most part, was well worn enough to easily navigate. Around noon, we reached the tributary on the map John had described. We stopped by the home of the McClearys to introduce ourselves as John recommended, and they showed us the best place to ford the river. The river was very calm and slow moving and not as John had described it, and I feared this was going to be a wasted trip. The McClearys explained the river had two forks, and if we crossed at the designated spot and stayed to the northwest, we would have to cross the river only once.

The small community John spoke about lay about two miles further north, they told us as we departed. As we continued, our spirits lifted. The northern fork of the river was much larger and swifter, and the water was crystal clear and cold, more to our liking. When we reached the community, it was nothing more than a few small houses and several outbuildings—nothing in comparison to the fort's dwellings, but closer to my expectations of wilderness homes: basic log cabins with shake roofs, no large glass windows or verandas. The thirty or so inhabitants, which included children, were a variety of British subjects and Indians. We explained the purpose of our trip and our relationship with John, and they invited us to bed down for the night, and one family graciously provided us with supper.

Early the next morning, they pointed us in the direction of John's place, and we headed off again with John's hand-drawn map as our guide. John said, from the community you will follow the river upstream; when you have crossed the second creek, you are getting close. When you reach the third creek, you are there. My place is about a mile further on.

When we reached the second creek, I could feel the emotion of the moment starting to well up. So much planning and traveling, obstacles, and doubt was about to come to a climax. Was all the hard work going to be worth the challenges we had faced? Everywhere we looked, there were trees, and the hillside rose gently at first and then more abruptly the further you traveled from the river. The area was a sea of trees, an ocean of green swaying in the wind. As we traveled east, the river made a sharp bend, and just as John had described it, the forest opened up, and we were standing at the edge of a meadow with golden grass as tall as my waist, except for a swath of green flowing through it. We stopped and listened, and we could hear the rush of water making its way to the river. You could hear it splashing against the rocks, and as we came closer, I could feel a soft mist of moisture on my face from the spray of the creek crashing against large rocks before it entered the river. We stopped and walked the horses to the edge of a ravine where we could finally see the waterfall, and the rainbow of color created by the sun reflecting on the falling shower of water.

After several minutes of breathlessness, we moved up the stream a couple hundred feet to a well-worn trail that crossed where the bank was low and easily passable. It was obvious this was the path to John's place. The open space of grassland unencumbered by trees had to be a quarter mile square; it was as if God had refused to let trees grow here. I kicked through the sod with my boot, and the soil looked dark and rich, as if it were ready for planting. I couldn't explain it, but it was as if it was already being used by someone.

We unsaddled the horses and turned them loose to feed as we made our way down to the river. The river was a couple of stone's throws in width and looked to average three to six feet in depth. It flowed unimpeded except for a natural outcropping of rocks ten to twelve feet wide that jutted out maybe twenty feet in to the river, which created a small cove of peaceful tranquility. It was here we peeled off our boots and socks, dangled our feet in the water, and took in our surroundings.

After a few moments of rest, we decided to make our way up the creek and into the hillside. From the open field where our horses continued to graze, the land rose steadily on both sides of the creek. There was a large grove of cedar trees on one side and towering fir trees on the other. About a quarter mile up, the stream forked. One fork disappeared into the denseness of trees that rose at a consistent climb for as far we could see; the second fork made its way around a hillside and up through a small valley. We decided to follow it. After a few hundred yards, we spotted a well-used deer trail, and we chose to see where it would take us. I could clearly see sunlight filtering through the trees as we climbed. We soon found ourselves at the edge of another open field with tall grass. We followed the tree line as it circled back towards the river. After a short hike, to our surprise, we found ourselves looking down on the field below where our horses were still grazing, and from our new vantage point, we could see there was a small path connecting them together. We continued to circle the tree line until we could see a small house and barn down below us, which we concluded was obviously John's place. I've seen enough, I said; what do you think, Sam, is this where we belong?

"It looks like home to me," he said, with a grin on his face.

We followed the ridge back to where we had entered it and descended back down to the creek. I wanted to determine one last thing before we left: where the best place for the waterwheel would be. We walked the stream for about a quarter mile up from the river and agreed the safest, easiest, and best place to create a diversion dam was near a small waterfall near the mouth of the creek. With our scouting finished, we caught the horses, saddled them up, and headed back for the fort. We agreed we would camp on the south side of the river where we had crossed the day before, and with an early start tomorrow, we could be back at the fort by early afternoon.

When we reached the fort the next day, Sam went to tell Mary all about the property. I went to see John. We talked at length about what Sam and I had seen, and he confirmed the house and the barn we had seen from the top of the hill was his. He said, "If you'd kept following the fork of the creek you started to traverse, it winds around the hillside and flows just behind my place. If you're set on settling there, you will need to make a written claim at the fort's record office before you leave. Have them write a statement you're claiming the square mile that borders the western edge of my place, and Sam is claiming the square mile next to you."

I said, "My brother is coming next year, and I'd like to have his property next to mine."

"Then tell the records office to leave a square mile between yours and mine, and your brother can claim it when he arrives. If you can contain your excitement and wait a few days, I'll have the work on this ship finished, and we can all travel back together. When we get back, I'll introduce you to my wife and children, and we can mark your property lines."

I said, "That sounds great. I need to buy a cow, a few chickens, and some other supplies from the fort store tomorrow, and we'll be ready to go."

He said, "Son, don't buy a cow. Wait until spring, so you don't have to feed it over the winter. Both of you can buy milk from me. It's going to take all the effort you have to build a place for your animals and yourself before the first winter storms and snow." I thanked him as I left. I turned and headed off to find Sam. I felt warm and happy. No one had called me son since my father had passed away.

Sam was still describing the property to Mary when I arrived. I explained to them what John had just related to me, and the most important thing was we needed to file our claims before we headed for our new home.

After our discussion, we proceeded to say our goodbyes to the friends with whom we had made the crossing. They were all headed to the Willamette Valley, and only the three of us were headed north. I said my goodbyes and best of wishes cordially, and then I slipped away as Sam and Mary continued their farewells. It was very hard for Mary to let go of these relationships. These were strong bonds forged in the throes of the constant daily battle to survive; tears were falling like rain everywhere. It wasn't that I hadn't bonded with my fellow travelers; it was I wanted to find John.

John was headed to supper when I caught up with him. The fort provided meals for most of their workers. He said, join me, there's always plenty of food for everyone. We grabbed a bowl of stew and several bread rolls and found a table. There were probably more than twenty men seated in the hall. I didn't realize I was so hungry, but I finished off two bowls of stew and half a dozen rolls as we talked. John said, "Don't make the mistake of trying to do everything at once. There is no way you're going to build a house before winter sets in. Do you have a shovel?"

"I have three Ames shovels, as well as picks and axes," I said.

"Good, well, when we get there, we'll scout out the best place to build a pit house and you can get started on it right away."

"What's a pit house?" I asked.

"A pit house is a hole in the ground," he said. "You dig a ten-to-twelve-foot circle five to six feet deep. You place a sturdy twelve-foot pole in the center, and then you build your teepee over the top of the hole, and it's an Indian winter home. You use a ladder to go in and out. The earth will help keep in the warmth. You can use the canvas from your wagon to cover your teepee poles, then build a wall of dirt several feet thick around the bottom of your teepee, to keep the wind from coming in and the teepee from blowing away. You can line your floor with rocks or wood planks. Just make sure you have nothing near your firepit that can catch on fire, and when you build a fire, it should be a small one, so you don't catch your teepee on fire. Next, you will need to get in your winter meat. There are plenty of deer and elk around, a couple of good-sized elk should give you plenty of meat. You can set some fishing lines as well and catch a dozen or so large winter steelhead to smoke along with your deer and elk meat.

"The most important shelter you will build is for your animals. It needs to be large enough for each animal to have a separate stall. Make it big enough that they can stand and turn around in it but not much more. I'd suggest you build it like a stockade with a lean-to roof. Don't make the roof flat. We get a lot of rain, and you want it to roll off as much as possible."

John said he'd be heading home in two days, and he'd meet us. He'd bring his family as well.

I returned to our campsite, and Sam and Mary were back. I shared what John had just told me. Sam said, I'm not living in a hole in the ground no matter how cold or wet it gets. The first thing on my list is to start building a house. We can stay in the wagon until I get it finished.

Not wanting to argue with him, I said okay. I will build a shelter for our animals, a pit house for myself, and kill a good supply of meat for all us for the winter. I then said good night; tomorrow's going to be a great day!

We were up early and ready to depart soon. We filed our land claims, and then began the last leg of our journey, to our new homes! My goal was to reach the McCleary place by late afternoon and stay the night there, then proceed to our new property in the morning.

When we arrived at the McCleary place, Mrs. McCleary came out and immediately grabbed Mary by the hand and took her into the house, while Sam and I took care of the wagons and animals. By the time we finished, Mary had returned with a warm apple pie—which Sam and I quickly consumed! I said, in a few years, I will hopefully have apples trees of my own, producing fruit! I brought starts from home.

We had dinner with the McClearys and then turned in for the evening. I slept very little, if any, before the sun came up. I was ready to travel within the hour. We said our goodbyes to the McClearys and started off, but not before we ate biscuits and jam, supplied by Mrs. McCleary.

In about an hour, we reached our new home!

We turned the horses and oxen loose to feed. I went down to the river, then made my way up the creek. Sam and Mary began their own exploring. I returned later to find they had moved their wagon across the creek and up a knoll to a small clearing that had a view of the river and the clearing down below. They said, this is where we are going to build our house and start our family! I said, I think I will dig my pit house down in the open field. They laughed!

A few hours later, John showed up with his wife and extended family. They were all Indians! I guess I was expecting a nice British family who sipped tea. They brought us some fresh eggs and milk. I asked John if he had any thoughts of where I should build my house and barn. So, John and I took a few minutes to scout out the best places. He took a look around and then said, I think this area would be the best. The weather tends to come from the west and the hillside here will block the wind, which will keep you and your animals warmer. I thanked John and his wife for the eggs and milk, but before we said our goodbyes, I said, you called this river the Lewis River; how many rivers are there in Oregon named after Meriwether Lewis? John said, this river is not named after Meriwether Lewis but after Lee Lewis, an early settler in the area.

> *The first recorded sighting of the Lewis River was in 1792, when William Robert Broughton passed the mouth of the river while exploring the Columbia River during the Vancouver Expedition. He named it Rushleigh's River at that time. At the time Lewis and Clark crossed the river, they had already named the Snake River after Meriwether Lewis, and referred to the present-day Lewis River as the Cathlapoote. When Adolphus Lee Lewis retired from the Hudson's Bay Company, he established a land claim near present-day Woodland, Washington, and applied his own name to the river.*

As soon as they were gone, Sam and I got to work. Our first task was to find a stand of trees twenty to twenty-five feet tall, with a diameter of about twelve inches. Within an hour, we had identified three small groves within a quarter mile that would satisfy our needs. Sam left me to join Mary, and I began unpacking my wagon. Soon, I had my axes, saws, and shovels unpacked, and I had chosen a place for my pit house and my barn. But after I thought about it more, I didn't want to smell the barn all night long; so I chose another place for my pit house further away from the barn and began digging.

The soil was sandy loam, easy to dig but not very stable. I could see right away I would need to fortify my pit house walls with timbers, to keep the walls from falling in on me. By the time I stopped for the day, I had completed a circle at a depth of nearly two feet. I ate a little food and headed to see what Sam had accomplished. They were eating when I arrived, so I ate again.

It was clear Sam had a much larger job than I. Before he could start on his home, he must first remove the trees and stumps from where he was going to build. I told him he could use two of my horses to help pull the stumps. But before I left, we made plans to fell several dozen trees and pull them back to my place for the next few days or until we had enough to meet our needs. I then said my goodbyes and headed back to my wagon. I actually slept in my wagon, instead of under it, for the first time since I'd left Independence.

Early the next morning, I met Sam, and we headed to the first stand of trees we had scouted the day before. By noon, we had more than a dozen trees cut and limbed. We took a break when Mary brought us lunch. When we finished lunch, I went back to my place and got two of my horses, harnesses, and ropes to begin dragging the logs back to my field, while Sam continued to fell trees. By day's end, we had a good start on the wood we would need initially. Before we called it a day, we agreed to continue logging for one more day. Day two of logging went about the same, except after lunch, Sam used the horses to drag the logs to the field, while I continued to fell trees.

On day three, Sam went back to pulling out stumps with help of my horses, while I continued digging my pit house. By day's end, I had my pit dug! On the other hand, Sam still had several more stumps to remove, and worse, he had saved the largest ones for last. It was a cold night, and when I awoke, the ground was covered with frost. The realization that cold winter weather was coming sooner than what we wanted forced both Sam and me to work harder and longer each day.

By the end of the week, I had my pit house structure finished. I decided to take two more days and use my wagon to haul rocks from the river to build my floor and fire pit. When finished, I placed the bed and small dresser I had brought from Independence in the pit—what I began to call my house—and lastly covered the pit with my teepee, originally my wagon cover. I built a fire and lay down in my bed. I rested about ten minutes before I was up again working. So much to do and very little time to complete it. I went back down to the river to wash my face, and set several fish lines. If I wasn't fully awake, after a splash of water from the river, I was—oh, it was cold!

With the pit finished, it was now time to build a shelter for our combined animals. I walked to the area John and I had agreed was best suited to protect the animals from the prevailing west wind. I did a bit of brush clearing, then sketched out on the ground a rough building plan. The next step would be to dig trenches three feet deep but only about a shovel's width wide. The good news was the soil was not sand but more stable. The bad news was it was harder to dig. My first thought was to build a twenty-by-twenty-foot shelter with interior walls. I quickly changed my mind and decided to a build a ten-by-thirty-foot shelter. By cutting down the width, I could eliminate the interior walls and save time. My next step was to figure about how many more trees I would need to fell to complete this building. It was about an hour before suppertime, so I decided to head back down to the river and check the fishlines I had set earlier. To my surprise, I had caught two nice-sized salmon. I took one back to the pit, and with the other in hand, I decided to check in on Sam and Mary's progress. Mary had supper already finished, but she thanked me for the salmon. I could see Sam's progress in removing stumps was slow, which was concerning. After supper, I thanked Mary for the diner and encouraged Sam in his struggle. I then headed back to my pit. My first night's sleep was the best I could remember!

Morning came early, but by midafternoon, I had completed the trench lines for my animal shelter. Drenched in sweat, I decided I would reset my fishlines while I took a cool bath in the river. As I soaked my sore muscles, I tried to estimate how many more days it would take to finish the shelter and how many more days before the first snow.

When John, being very neighborly, dropped by with more eggs, I asked him about it. He said, "I have good news and bad news for you. The first snow can happen any time after mid-November. The good news is it doesn't usu-ally last more than a day. The heavy snows won't arrive until after the first of the year. The worst snows arrive between late January and early February, but they don't usually last more than a week!"

Being from Missouri, I thought that's not so bad; so what's the bad news?

He said, "From now until late April, it can rain all day, every day, for weeks at a time!" He looked at me and said, "You look stunned. Why do you think we have these huge, beautiful evergreen trees and clear swift streams"!

All I knew was, in Missouri, winter meant it was cold, sometimes very cold, and nearly all the precipitation falls as snow. No one, including Rev. Lee, mentioned in Oregon there would be days, sometimes weeks on end, of cold rain!

After my visit with John, I took half the eggs up to Mary and Sam and shared the news about what we should expect for weather this winter. When I told them, I could see Sam's head drop. He had been working so hard, and this was not good news. Before I left, I told him I would be finished with the animal shelter in twelve to fourteen days, and then I could start helping him.

I finished the animal shelter in ten days. By my count, it was now mid-Oc-tober. The animals were now warm and dry, and Sam had finally removed all his stumps and leveled his building site. However, it had been raining for the last two days, very hard at times.

I now turned my attention to making sure the three—I mean, the four— of us would have enough food for the winter. I killed a large elk, and John helped me dry the meat, teaching me how, so I could do it myself the next time, which was as soon as we had finished the lessons. Within two weeks, I had enough deer, elk, and salmon smoked to last us through the winter, and with the eggs and milk supplied by John, I felt we could survive the winter, maybe even enjoy ourselves. After all, Sam and Mary were expecting a child sometime in April!

Sam was now making good progress on their log home. He had the walls almost finished and would soon be putting on the roof. We spent one more day felling and dragging a few more trees to his site before I left. I had one more important job to complete and that was to make sure our animals didn't starve. They had eaten nearly all the vegetation available, and with the winter setting in would be dependent on grain feed for the next several months. So, I decided I would make my way to Fort Vancouver and buy as much grain as I could haul in my wagon or as much as they would sell me. The day I left, the sun was shining, although the temperature was cool. My expectation was it would be a three-day trip, and by the time I got back, Sam and Mary would have a roof on their house.

I arrived at the fort and immediately went to see John. I filled him in on Sam's progress and asked him how much I should pay for the grain. He said, they will want a half-dollar a sack; but tell them some of it's for me, and they will give it to you for thirty-five cents a sack. Which they did!

On the way back, the clouds parted, and I could see the sun. I was feeling joyous. Life was good: come spring, Daniel and Whitney would be on their way to join me, Sam and I would have the sawmill up and running, I wouldn't be living in the pit, Mary would have her baby, and Whitney and I would get married soon!

All that joyous feeling soon disappeared when I arrived home the next day. I found Mary crying hysterically and Sam lying in the back of their wagon with his right leg bandaged heavily. I could see immediately it was bad. The wrap on his leg was soaked in blood, and he was in and out of consciousness. Mary explained, through her tears, Sam was chopping a log, when his axe glanced off the log and split open his leg. I said, we need to take Sam to see the doctor at the fort now. I unloaded my wagon as fast as I could and returned for Sam and Mary.

We needed to cross the river before dark or we'd have to wait until morning, I told Mary. Once we cross the river, we can travel even through the darkness. We crossed the river and continued as fast as we could. We arrived at the fort early the next morning and immediately got help to carry Sam to the infirmary. Dr. McLoughlin came immediately. After attending to the wound and bandaging it properly, he came to see us. He said, "Sam's lost a lot of blood, but my biggest concern is fever. We should know more by this evening." He then invited us both to his home, fed us breakfast, and gave us a place to rest. Mary had been awake for nearly a day. She rested but not well. As soon as I had Mary settled, I went to talk with Dr. McLoughlin once again. I asked him how soon before we would know something. He said we'll watch his fever: if it climbs higher, or if the wound starts to discharge fluid, those will be signs he's not doing well.

> Dr. McLoughlin (chief factor at Fort Vancouver) began to study medicine under Sir James Fisher of Quebec in 1798. In 1803, McLoughlin was granted a license to practice medicine in Lower Canada (now Quebec). He was hired as a physician at Fort William, the inland headquarters and fur trade post of the North West Company on Lake Superior.

Dr. McLoughlin came to see us in the late afternoon. He said, "Sam is slipping away. His fever is extremely high. My guess is he has only a few more hours." Mary went to see him immediately. She sat by his side and held his hand, but Sam had no reaction. Then, in the late hours, Sam opened his eyes and asked for a drink of water. They kissed and told each other how much they loved each other. They talked about special memories, then Sam lapsed again. He passed away in the early morning hours with Mary, myself, and Dr. Mcloughlin by his side.

My fear was for Mary and the baby, but Mary showed me she was a strong woman, at least on the outside. We stayed at the fort one more day before we headed home to bury Sam. Dr. McLoughlin sent John with us. We stopped at the McCleary place and shared the news. Mrs. McCleary and her husband dropped everything and followed as well. Mary chose a place, and John and I dug a grave. The next morning, we said our farewells to Sam.

Mrs. McCleary wanted Mary to come home with her, but she said she wanted to stay with me. I wasn't sure what the future was going to look like, but I promised Sam I'd take care of Mary and their child.

After everyone left, I went and brought Mary's wagon down to my place. I asked her what she needed, and I brought her down into the pit. I had expected to be living alone, not sharing my makeshift winter home. I had not lived with anyone but my brother for years, and Whitney always went home before it was time to go to bed. The pit was not big enough for two beds, so I slept in a sitting-up position against the wall. But after two nights, Mary asked me to please sleep next to her.

A few days later, she shared her plan was to wait until the baby was born in the spring, and when the child was old enough to travel safely, she would return to the East Coast by ship, if she could raise the money. I told her, if that was what she wanted, I would help her raise the money, I was sure we could sell her land claim for at least that much, especially if we finished the log house.

After a few days rest, I explained to Mary I felt our best choice would be to finish the house Sam had started—which only made her cry, but after a few moments, she agreed. She said, "If we don't, in another month, I will be so big, you'll have to sleep on the floor again!"

For a few days, I worked just by myself. I was able to get the roof completed, and I had started to collect stones for a fireplace when Mary joined me in the endeavor. The news spread quickly and within a few more days, John and his family, the McClearys, and two men Mr. McLoughlin had sent to help had the house finished. It was still only one room, but at least we had separate beds, a real fireplace for heat, and a small cookstove Dr. McLoughlin sent as a gift. We were now more or less set for the winter, and with no time to spare. Within days of moving in, it rained for a week straight, followed by an early snow!

The snow didn't last the day, but it was a harbinger of what was to come. We had plenty of firewood and dried meat but lacked other items. I dropped Mary off at Mrs. McCleary's and headed with my wagon to Fort Vancouver, where I purchased four fifty-pound sacks of potatoes, two hundred pounds of flour, and an assortment of other items from Mary's list. I then returned to the McClearys to pick up Mary. Mary had secured a number of canned items from local residents, which included carrots, peaches, and applesauce. I now felt we could survive the next two or three months without purchasing more supplies. We could also count on fresh fish, according to John.

The daylight hours were becoming shorter each week and the temperature cooler, so we concentrated on the daily chores, making sure the animals got exercise, food, and water. There was plenty of firewood chopped and, whenever possible, long walks. I played my fiddle every now and then, but not too often, and we read to each other from the books I had brought. Before we knew it, it was Christmas!

My memories of the holidays have always been special, not because of the gifts, of which most were clothes, but more because of the traditions. Before my father passed away, we always gathered as an extended family and we'd take turns reading from the Bible about the birth of Jesus—even if it was just one sentence, with help from Mother. So, when I suggested to Mary we read from the family Bible my mother had given to me, and she said no, I was hurt. I wasn't sure how to react until she started crying and said, I don't know how to read.

"I don't know how to read, my parents didn't know how to read, and Sam could barely read. Almost as soon as I could walk, I was put to work in the fields. My parents never read the Bible to me, and we never went to church. I have no fond memories of Christmas until I married Sam, and now, I don't have him!" Neither of us said anything for the longest time. I just held her as she cried.

I finally got up and went to retrieve my family Bible. I told her, you can just listen, as I read from the book of Matthew, starting with verse eighteen.

> Now the birth of Jesus Christ was on this wise: When as his mother Mary was espoused to Joseph, before they came together, she was found with child of the Holy Ghost. Then Joseph her husband, being a just man, and not willing to make her a publick example, was minded to put her away privily. But while he thought on these things, behold, the angel of the Lord appeared to him in a dream, saying, Joseph, thou son of David, fear not to take unto thee Mary thy wife: for that which is conceived in her is of the Holy Ghost. And she shall bring forth a son, and thou shalt call his name JESUS: for he shall save his people from their sins. Now all this was done, that it might be fulfilled which was spoken of the Lord by the prophet, saying, Behold, a virgin shall be with child, and shall bring forth a son, and they shall call his name Emmanuel, which being interpreted is, God with us. Then Joseph being raised from sleep did as the angel of the Lord had bidden him, and took unto him his wife: And knew her not till she had brought forth her firstborn son: and he called his name JESUS.

After I finished, I told her, you are named after Jesus's mother. I asked her if she would like to read one sentence if I helped. She said, I don't know words. I said, it's okay, just repeat after me, and follow my finger as I touch them.

And—he—called—his—name—Jesus.

I said, "I don't know how every word is written, but I remember many from memorizing them."

Mary said, "I would like to learn to read, so I can teach my child."

"Would you like to continue?"

"Please!"

I turned my Bible to the New Testament book of John, chapter three, verse sixteen. I said, "This is how my Mother started me. I memorized each word, so when I saw it used other places, I knew it. I will say the word first and then you repeat it."

For—God—so—loved—the—world—that—he—gave—his—only—begotten—Son—that—who—so—ever—believeth—in—him—should—not—perish—but—have—everlasting—life.

After Mary finished, I smiled at her. "You just read for the first time! Sam would be proud of you!" From that day forward, she learned new words and verses each day.

January brought rain and more rain but no snow. That changed in February. We woke up one morning to find several inches of snow covering the ground, and it didn't stop until it was several feet, days later.

I made a trail to the animals and let them out each day. The good news is they remained healthy, and the bad news is we were running out of grain faster than I expected. I talked with Mary about selling her oxen team. We didn't need them, it would be fewer animals to feed, and she would need the money.

Once the snow had melted, we decided to make a trip to Fort Vancouver to buy more supplies and sell the oxen and for Mary to have a check-up with Dr. McLoughlin.

Dr. McLoughlin said Mary was doing well, as was the baby. Mary was able to get a good price for the oxen team. We spent one night at the fort and headed home the next day with a wagon filled with supplies and feed.

For the next few weeks, the days were cool but dry, and I was able to get some work done outside. I constructed a fence, which allowed the animals to get out and move around freely.

Just when it felt like winter might be over, things changed again quickly. The wind changed from coming from the west, to coming from the north. The temperature plummeted—no snow, just bone-chilling days. So much so, the Columbia River froze several inches thick, enough thickness to support the weight of several large men. The Lewis River, on the other hand, moved much too fast to freeze over.

To our surprise, John stopped by to see if we wanted to go ice-skating! The McClearys have invited us to join them, he said; the locals are skating completely across the river to the opposite shore. We decided to join them. Mary watched with Mrs. McCleary while I made a fool of myself. Ice skates and I were not meant for each other, so before I broke an arm or leg. I joined several others as a spectator instead of as a participant.

March came in like a lamb. It was, for the most part, warm and dry. More importantly, I was able to start working on building the sawmill. I chose a location and began the process of construction. My first task was to build the foundation the waterwheel would sit in, which meant I needed to be able to make cement. I had brought lime and gypsum with me from Missouri. I now needed to find a supply of clay, ash, and sand. The last two items were not a problem; what I needed to find was a supply of clay. I headed to see John. If anyone could point me in the right direction, I knew he could. I was right. We walked down to the river about a quarter mile from his place and he dug up a shovel of solid clay. He said, "I'm sure if you clear off the plant growth around here, you will find more than enough for your needs, as well as a supply to fill the cracks between logs on your cabin."

I now had what I needed. I framed the two pillars the waterwheel would sit on, I secured a sleeve in each pillar for the wheel's axle, and I poured each frame with my mixture of concrete. After three days, I removed the forms. It looked good—another week, and I could start the construction of the wheel.

Not wanting to waste time, I unpacked the boards I would use to construct the wheel and laid them out according to my blueprint. With that finished, I began digging the diversion trench and lining it with rocks. The trench starts wide and then narrows the closer it gets to the wheel, giving the water greater force.

By the time I had completed the trench, the cement's color had turned from a dark green-gray to a light gray, indicating it was curing well. I could now build the wheel. Mary supervised and kept me company, double-checking the blueprint as I put together the jigsaw puzzle. It took two days to finish, but when we were done, it was a sight to behold. To test it, I opened the diversion trench and let the water flow: the trench filled, and the wheel began to turn, just as it was supposed to. The next step would be to assemble the mill.

But when I woke up the next morning, the weather had another idea. It was raining harder than I had ever seen. Mary said, "Welcome to spring in Oregon."

After two days, the rain stopped for the immediate future, and while the sky was not blue, at least the sky wasn't falling. The end of the month had arrived, and Mary's due date was just around the corner. Not wanting to take any chances, we decided it was time she should move to the McClearys' home until after her child's birth and her recovery. I helped pack her things and carried them to the wagon, then returned to help her onto the wagon. She talked and I listened, for the most part, until we reached the McCleary home. I helped her down and carried her things into the house. Mrs. McCleary said they'd send word when the child was born. I said goodbye and headed home. A few days turned into a week, and one week into two. Then the word came, Mary had given birth!

I saddled up a horse and followed the messenger, Mr. McCleary, back to his home. I was somewhat concerned, because he hadn't said much about the health of Mary or the child. When we arrived, I acted reserved, but I felt like I was dancing on pins and needles.

Mrs. McCleary came out the bedroom, smiling, and said, "Mary is ready to see you." I entered the room and she was lying in bed, smiling, with her child in her arms. She said, "Thomas, I would like you to meet Samuel." He has eyes just like his father, I said; he's beautiful. She then gave Samuel to Mrs. McCleary, and she laid him in his crib, then returned. She handed Mary the baby again, and Mary said, "Thomas, I would like you to meet Anna."

I was speechless, until it finally came out: "Twins!"

Mary said, "Yes!"

I left very happy, knowing Mary and the children were healthy. Mary stayed another week at the McClearys' before she returned home. Mary had her hands full with two babies, so I became a surrogate father. But I also had work to accomplish. Before Mary and Sam had agreed to join me, my plan was to accomplish what had to be done on my own. That's what I had planned and trained for, and once again, it was my reality. It was now mid-April, which left me about six months to prepare for Whitney and Daniel's arrival.

It took me a couple of days, but I finished the waterwheel, and with the help of John and his young son, we accomplished setting up the sawmill. As a test, we placed a few logs on the platform and released the waterwheel. Once the blade was spinning sufficiently, I moved a log into place and began the cut. With a little adjustment, the blade cut the log perfectly. I ran the log threw three more times until I had perfectly honed six-inch-square timber. John said, "Young man, I believe you are in business! I will have an order for you within a week, along with the dimensions." As John and his son walked away, I ran to tell Mary the news.

I was determined not to wait for John's order and began the next day felling and dragging logs to the mill. By week's end, I had a sufficient stockpile to begin cutting. Not knowing what dimensions or lengths, I cut the logs into twelve-inch squares. By the time John arrived a week later with order in hand, I had forty timbers ready to be sized.

When John arrived, he said, "I not only have my order for you, but I have a minister who wants to talk to you. He has just arrived and plans to build a church in the new community on the Willamette River called Portland."

It took a few more days, and I had John's order ready. My plan was to take Mary and the children to stay with the McClearys for a few days while I delivered the order to the fort and made contact with the new minister, Rev. James Wilbur.

When I got to the fort, I was surprised: Dr. McLoughlin was entertaining Rev. Wilbur. I asked where I should unload the lumber, to which Dr. McLoughlin said, I'll have someone do that for you, if would like to join us for some refreshments. He then introduced me to Rev. Wilbur. Dr. McLoughlin said, "I think you two have much in common, if my memory serves me correctly. You are both Methodist; you, Mr. Merriman, now own a sawmill, and Rev. Wilbur wants to build a church." We talked about many things but mostly why we had come to Oregon. Before I left, Rev. Wilbur and I shook hands and agreed to work together on building his church. We agreed to meet in one week at my sawmill. He would bring his building plans and a list of needed lumber by size and count.

I also collected a twenty-dollar gold piece for my lumber. It was British coin, but I didn't care. The only place to spend it was at the Hudson's Bay Company store at Fort Vancouver. The last thing I did was purchase a bolt of cloth and supply of thread for Mary, so she could sew some outfits for the twins and a dress for herself.

> *Known as Father Wilbur, the energetic and determined Rev. James Harvey Wilbur was a leader in Oregon's early Methodist community. He established a number of Methodist institutions in Oregon and later moved to the Yakama Indian Reservation, where he spent twenty years as a missionary and Indian agent. In Portland, he was the first minister of the Taylor Street Methodist Episcopal Church. He built a simple wood-framed church for the congregation, reportedly doing much of the physical labor himself. He also oversaw construction of the Portland Academy and Female Seminary, the first school in the city to offer elementary and secondary education.*

When I returned home, I shared with Mary about meeting Rev. Wilbur and presented her with the cloth and sewing supplies. Mr. Wilbur kept his appointment, and we agreed upon a price. We divided the order into thirds, with the first shipment due in forty-five days. I agreed to take the lumber to the mouth of the Lewis River where it meets the Columbia River; he agreed to have a ship pick it up there.

For the next two weeks, I worked from sunup to sundown felling trees and dragging them to the mill. Mary convinced me I needed a day of rest, to which I agreed.

By the time my feet hit the floor, Mary had a breakfast of hotcakes and eggs waiting for me. As I ate, she informed me of my plans for the day. After I finished eating, I was to watch the children while she bathed and washed clothes; then we were going to take a picnic lunch down to the river and enjoy each other's company, which we did—and it was enjoyable. As we sat on a blanket by the river, with the sun warming our skin, I realized I wasn't the one who needed a break, and I kept that in mind as the summer unfolded.

Before we left, I skipped a few rocks across the river. To my surprise, I found several Indian arrowheads.

Two weeks later, I stepped out of our cabin in the morning to find the large open field below us covered in teepees. They were not there the night before! Suddenly, I realized why this large open field of grassland existed; it was an Indian campground. I had no more called to Mary to come see this when I recognized John coming up the hill. I asked, what's going on?

"It's summer fishing time. Groups of Yakama Indians have been coming here for generations. They are part of my wife's and her family's people. The men will fish with spears, the women will build fires and dry the salmon, and the children will pick blackberries and huckleberries. When they have what they need, they will celebrate with a great feast and games, then return back across the mountains."

"How did they get here, and how long before they leave?" I asked, and "Are they angry I have taken their land?"

John said, "No, no, they're not angry with you. First, they got here by walking, and they will be happy as long as they can stay here!"

"Okay. How long before they leave?"

"About a month," John said.

John introduced me to their chief, who happened to be John's wife's uncle. He wanted to know all about my sawmill, so I showed him how it worked. He was amazed. They did just as John said they would: the men speared the fish, and the women dried the fish. I watched as the men lined up nearly shoulder to shoulder across a shallow part of the river. If the salmon hadn't been so plentiful, none would have made it through their human net.

If I hadn't had a promise to keep, I would have interacted with them more; but because I did have one, I continued to work each day at the sawmill, watching at a distance the activities going on in my field.

After two weeks, the men stopped fishing, but the women continued working. The men now began to play. They held races to determine the fastest men and wrestled to determine the strongest. But mostly, they ate. Then one morning, I got up, and they were gone.

By the 4th of July, I had Rev. Wilbur's initial order finished. All I needed to do was to get it to the Columbia River. The problem was most of the beams were much longer than a wagon bed. I finally figured it out: if I centered the beams on the wagon and strapped them down tightly, it would work, but it also meant I had to lead the horses by walking. It took twelve trips, but the solution worked. I now had about three months to build a home for myself and Whitney.

I chose a place about a hundred yards east of the sawmill and about the same distance south of the animal shelter. I wanted it to be a two-bedroom house with wood floors, a large living room with windows and a fireplace, an open kitchen, and a dining room. The front of the house would have a full-length covered porch for enjoying the evening hours. I staked it out and began taking measurements. This would not be a log cabin with a dirt floor, like the one Mary, the children, and I were living in now; it would be a cut timber home on a masonry foundation.

After making sure the outline was square, I was ready to start the foundation. I didn't have bricks, but I had plenty of river rock. I took my wagon down to the river and began very selectively choosing the size and shape of each stone. I took a week to select and haul all the rocks I needed and another two weeks to build a solid foundation. It was now early August, and I needed to cut and deliver the next part of Reverend Wilbur's order. It took me until the end of August to complete it, but this time there would be no ship to pick it up. I would need to deliver it by wagon to Fort Vancouver, where he would pick it up, which would require at least six or seven trips, and each round trip would take at least two days. It was clear I needed to secure some help. I talked to John and Mr. McCleary, and they both agreed to haul one load, which they did—and I paid them well for it—and by the end of the week, we were finished. I now had plenty of money, but I was running out of time. Daniel and Whitney would be here soon. I was becoming desperate. I finally told Mary, "I don't see how I will be ready in time."

She said, "We will do the best we can, and we will all survive. If we have to, we can all stay here in this home. By spring, the children should be ready to travel, and by next summer, you will have the home finished you and Whitney have always wanted."

I knew she was right, but suddenly I felt sad. I had grown fond of the children. While what she said made sense, I had always hoped she would change her mind and stay here in Oregon. I continued to work on my house, but I knew we would need to implement the secondary plan.

September came and went, and there was no word from Daniel and Whitney. Then a week later, word came through John: they had arrived at Fort Vancouver. I was overjoyed. Mary, the children, and I dropped everything and left immediately. It had been seventeen months since we had seen each other.

When we arrived at the fort, we asked for their location. There were groups of wagons huddled in multiple locations. While I waited for an answer, I turned around, and there stood Daniel. He had grown so much. He was not the boy I had left in Missouri but a full-grown man. After we hugged, he said, I need to talk to you.

Suddenly my heart sank. Had something happened to Whitney; had she changed her mind and not come?

I looked into his eyes as his tears began to fall. He said, "We never intended for this to happen, I'm not even sure how it happened—more importantly, neither one of us wants to hurt you!"

"What is it, Daniel?" I said. "Whitney and I love each other; we plan to get married."

By now, Daniel was crying uncontrollably. "We never intended to hurt you," he kept repeating.

"It's okay," I said, "Everything is going to be okay. Don't leave. I need to speak to someone. God always works things out for the best."

I ran to see Mary, who I was sure must have begun to worry.

When I reached her, I said, "I know you loved Sam very much. Do you think you could love me?"

She said, "What's happening?"

I said, "I love you and the children: do you think you could love me?"

"I'm not sure what is happening here," she said, "but if you are telling me you love me . . ."

"I am," I said.

"Then, yes, I love you, yes, I love you!"

I explained what had happened.

We both then went to see Daniel and Whitney.

The next day, the four of us crossed the river and made our way to meet Rev. Wilbur. After a long explanation, Daniel and Whitney said their wedding vows, and then Mary and I said ours.

After the brief ceremonies, Rev. Wilbur spoke. He said, what a day, in matter of a few hours, you've gone from being single to married with a family. I said, God can move in mysterious ways. True, he said: with God, I've learned to always expect the unexpected!

CHAPTER 5

∞∞

And the Wagons Kept On Coming

I WOULD INTERVIEW THOMAS three more times before he died. The first time, we covered the years between Daniel and Whitney's arrival and the Civil War.

News of wagon trains reaching Oregon and California successfully in 1841 and 1842 began to spread like wild fire. Letters sent back to family members, like the ones sent by Thomas Merriman to Whitney and Daniel, confirmed it: while the journey was arduous, the possibilities were endless. The promise of free land, new opportunities, and dreams fueled continuous migrations. One of the largest, historically, became known as the Great Migration. It's estimated as many as a thousand emigrants followed the trail to Oregon in 1843, and they kept coming by wagon until modern railroads became the chosen form of transportation.

> *Over the years, military posts, trading posts, shortcuts, and spur roads sprang off the Oregon Trail. And then the railroad reached the Far West. The Central Pacific Railroad connected California to the rest of the continent in 1869. The Oregon Shortline finished a railroad in 1884 from the Union Pacific Railroad in Wyoming to Huntington, Oregon. Wagon trains gave way to modern transportation, and the trail became mostly a route for eastward cattle drives.*

One of the things I always enjoyed in talking with Thomas was the way he communicated. He always seemed to get to the heart of the question.

What happened after the marriages?

After we were married, the six of us returned to our place on the Lewis River. We all moved into Mary's home, while Daniel and I worked to finish the home I had started, which would now become Daniel and Whitney's home.

What did you do with the windows you brought from Missouri?

I told Mary about how I had brought windows from Missouri for Whitney and asked her what she thought I should do with them. She said, give them to Whitney; you can buy new ones for me! We both laughed.

As luck would have it, the rain held off for the most part, until the end of October—long enough for the basic structure to be livable. Daniel and Whitney moved in immediately—I don't know why—probably for the same reason Mary and I couldn't wait for them to leave.

With the house finished, Daniel and I concentrated on fulfilling the last part of Rev. Wilbur's order. I prayed the winter weather would hold off as long as possible. We also had several small orders to fill and a large order from the fort.

Times were changing, and Dr. McLoughlin could see it. He continued to encourage all the new settlers to settle south of the Columbia River. But with each new migration group, more chose to settle north of the river. In 1842, three new families settled in the Lewis River Valley, and two other families settled even further north at the confluence of the Columbia River and the Cowlitz River.

Two of the new families made land claims near the McClearys; the other family settled just beyond John's property. So, we had new neighbors.

In 1843, nearly a hundred more new settlers chose to settle at the mouth of the Cowlitz River, and others moved even further north, a few as far north as Puget Sound.

> *Puget Sound was named after Peter Puget who was a lieutenant under George Vancouver and who explored the inland waterways of northwest Washington.*

Why were people settling further north?

The first reason was presidential candidate James Polk was running for office with the slogan "Fifty-four Forty or Fight!" Manifest destiny was again at the forefront of U.S. politics, and the United States was pushing for settlement as far north as possible.

The second was prejudice. I was at Fort Vancouver when George Washington Bush's small wagon train arrived. I was surprised such a small group of people would attempt the journey on their own; most wagon trains by this time had between fifty to a hundred wagons or more. But I soon understood: George Washington Bush and his family were black.

In an instant, my thoughts were taken back to Mr. Sowers's store, the young black slave, and Yankee. I introduced myself and asked the small party what their plans were. They said they were looking for a place to settle. I told them about the Lewis River Valley and asked if they would like to visit the area. They asked how many lived in the valley, and I told them very few. They talked with each other and decided at least to visit the area. So, they followed me north.

I made my usual stop, and Mrs. McCleary whipped up something for us to eat. But before we had finished our meal, a small but vocal group of men and women had gathered outside the McCleary home demanding to know the party's plans. When I explained they were looking for a place to settle, several people shouted, "Not here, move on!"

I felt ashamed and angry, but Mr. Bush quickly answered, "We wish only to spend the night and then we will be moving on in the morning."

I tried to dissuade him, but he said, "We will go, God will give us a home, where we can be safe and wanted." I stayed with them for the night and wished them well as they left. I felt even more ashamed, and I limited my interaction from that day forward with those whom I felt had behaved so unchristianly that day.

Mr. Bush and his party established a home at the southern tip of the Puget Sound in what is modern-day Tumwater, Washington.

> *The Bush-Simmons Party is credited by some historians as being responsible for bringing the land north of the Columbia River into the United States.*

Between 1843 and 1847, most immigrants moving into the Oregon Territory north of the Columbia River settled further north than the mouth of the Cowlitz River, due to pressure and interference from the Hudson's Bay Company. In 1847, three settlers did move into the area, and we quickly became friends. I furnished the lumber used in the construction of all three men's homes. Owen Bozarth established a land claim a few miles above the mouth of the Lewis River and would play a significant role in the establishment of the community of Woodland, while Mr. Crawford and Mr. Rayner settled on opposite sides of the Cowlitz River where the river meets the Columbia.

After the Great Migration of 1843, the numbers remained high but fell off after 1847.

Why?

Two reasons, the first being safety. In late 1847, a measles outbreak hit the Whitman Mission. One of the white settlers passing through to the Willamette Valley brought the disease with them. They passed the disease on to others at the mission, including the child of an indian chief. When the chief's son died, he blamed Dr. Whitman. As retaliation, the chief led an attack against the mission, killing Dr. Whitman, his wife, and eleven other people. The unrest caused fear, and fewer settlers chose to migrate to Oregon.

> *Even in the midst of the measles outbreak and the Native American unrest, political changes were taking place. On August 14, 1848, Congress established the Oregon Territory.*

The second reason was gold. It was discovered in California, and the rush was no longer to Oregon but to California.

Did the gold rush impact you?

Greatly. Cut lumber was in huge demand, and sources even as far north as the Puget Sound, including my mill, were impacted. In both 1849 and 1850, we shipped large amounts of lumber to San Francisco. We set up a storage area at the mouth of the Lewis River, where ships could load our lumber. It was the same place Rev. Wilbur had picked up supplies previously.

In 1850, I had this great idea. Instead of hauling all the lumber by wagon to the Columbia River, we'd float it down the Lewis River and take it out of the river before it entered the Columbia River.

How did that work out?

Not well. My idea was to create a necklace made of logs by tying all the logs together with rope. This would create an open space in the center where we could place all the cut lumber. We would then float the necklace down the river and pull all the lumber out when it reached the Columbia River.

What happened?

The necklace broke apart halfway there, and the lumber began floating away uncontrollably. Some got stuck along the shoreline, and some floated into the Columbia before we could catch it. Eventually, we collected probably seventy-five percent of it, but it took more time than if we'd had hauled it all by wagon.

Did you have any other bright ideas?

Yes, and one worked. Instead of pulling all the logs to the mill with a team of horses, we built a flume, which allowed us to float the logs to the mill. Once the flume was built, it paid for itself a hundred times over or more and doubled our production.

I understand you became friends with Ben Snipes during this time?

Ben was a dreamer, a great dreamer! He was living in Iowa when gold was discovered in California. Like most, he came to the party late and was soon broke. He survived by getting a job as a butcher. But he still had gold fever, and when gold was discovered on the Fraser River in British Columbia, he headed north. I met him at Fort Vancouver. He was looking for a job. He worked for Daniel and me for a few weeks, then headed north again.

When he reached the Fraser River, once again, he was too late. All the likely claims had been taken. But he realized there was another opportunity available, other than striking gold. There were thousands of men, many with pockets full of gold, but lacking food, especially meat. Men afraid to leave their claims because of claim jumpers. Ben realized he could make money by driving cattle to the area and selling beef to the miners.

Ben quickly returned south. He worked again for us for a few days, then he headed further south, to find a cattleman who would be willing to let him drive part of his herd north to sell to the miners. The rest is history. Ben not only made the cattleman a small fortune, he made enough of a stake to fund his own future cattle drives.

> *Ben Snipes was known as the Cattle King. By 1861, he had an estimated 25,000 to 40,000 head of cattle.*

I understand you became politically minded during this time?

No one was happier than I when Reverend Lee's dream had finally come to fruition with the establishment of the Oregon Territory, but those of us who lived north of the Columbia River were unhappy when the territorial capital was established in Salem. Many began pushing for the establishment of a separate territory north of the river.

The movement gained strength, starting in 1851, and caught fire during the Independence Day celebration in Olympia. Word spread quickly that all communities on the north side of the Columbia should send representatives to a convention to be held at Cowlitz Landing the following month. I volunteered to go to the first convention at Cowlitz Landing, and a second convention held later at Monticello, as a representative of the Lewis River Valley.

> *Cowlitz Landing was located near present-day Toledo, Washington, in Lewis County. The second meeting, from which the convention and petition took their names, took place in the town of Monticello, later destroyed by flooding in 1867. It was later replaced by the present-day city of Longview, Washington, in Cowlitz County.*
>
> *The first meeting of settlers on August 29, 1851, met to draft a petition to Congress to create a new territory north of the Columbia River. Seth Catlin, a former Illinois legislator, was elected president of the convention. Taking two days, a document was prepared explaining their demands to Congress and why they needed Congress's support. The document was a fifteen-hundred-word "Memorial to Congress" listing the problems and issues facing those living north of the Columbia River.*

> *Still feeling ignored by the Oregon Territory government, forty-four delegates met on November 25, 1852, to develop, complete, and sign another petition to have the Columbia Territory established. Although this memorial was shorter than the earlier Cowlitz Memorial, it was better written (the 1851 document focused too much on ills of the Hudson's Bay Company and not enough on the problems of settlers north of the Columbia River not being addressed by the Oregon Territorial Government) and quickly adopted. After the petition was signed, it was again forwarded to Joseph Lane, who supported the petition and had it sent on to Congress.*

The result was the creation of the Washington Territory in 1853. Many in Congress felt the nation owed a huge debt to George Washington and believed a state should be named in his honor.

So, what happened next?

The federal government appointed Isaac Stevens governor of the new Washington Territory, and his first assigned task was to negotiate treaties with the Indians on both sides of the Cascade Mountains and to move the Indians on to reservations. In return for signing the treaties, the Indians were to receive half of the fish in the territory in perpetuity, awards of money and provisions, and reserved lands where white settlement would be prohibited.

John was very distraught. Under the treaty with the Yakamas, John's wife's family members would no longer be able to visit. And the creation of the Washington Territory had forced the Hudson's Bay Company to move its operation north to Vancouver Island. But John was determined to stay. I told him, everyone in this valley knows you and your family, and you are part of this valley's family. But I was wrong!

The ink was barely dry when the discovery of gold on the Yakama Reservation prompted an influx of unruly prospectors, who traveled unchecked across the newly defined tribal lands. In 1855, two of these prospectors were killed after it was discovered they'd raped a Yakama woman. The new territory was in turmoil, and the U.S. Army was called upon to put down the uprising. But the Yakama Indians were proving themselves to be a mighty foe.

In March 1856, members of the Yakama tribe crossed the mountains and were making their way down the Lewis River with the intent of burning the homes of settlers. The plan was thwarted because of "Indian Zack," a member of the Cowlitz tribe who warned the settlers ahead of time. For some unknown reason, some settlers blamed John.

By the end of 1857, John had had enough. He sold his land claim to me and moved his family to Vancouver Island.

As the uprising entered its third year, the U.S. Army was at a loss. They lacked knowledge of the land and were not well equipped. It was not until the advent of new long range rifles that they successfully defeated the Yakamas and other tribes of the Pacific Northwest.

The Civil War broke out in 1861. How did it impact you?

The war didn't have as much of an impact as you might think. But after the war was over, there was an impact.

What kind of impact?

New settlers began moving into the valley, refuges from the war. Most were not from the North but from the South, and many were angry and hurting on the inside. They came for the land, but they brought their prejudice with them. Nearly all previous settlers were living on the north side of the river; but after the war, many new settlers took up claims on the south side of the river valley. The river was not much more than two stone's throws in width across, but it might as well have been miles across. For years, it seemed like there was no common ground.

What changed?

Time and a small schoolhouse. They say time heals all wounds, and with education comes enlightenment. By the late 1860s, the majority of families on both sides of the river had children. Mary said to me one morning, "We should build a schoolhouse."

I said, "Don't you think we should first build a church?"

She said, why not build a building that could be used as both.

Together, we chose a nice flat parcel of land that had once belonged to John, near the wagon road that now extended more than fifteen miles up the Lewis River from the mouth of the Columbia. The news of what we were building spread quickly, and with the help of other families, we soon had both a church and a schoolhouse started. I contacted Rev. Wilbur about the possibility the Methodists might provide us with a minister. He wrote back, he had a young woman who would soon be finished with her education who would be willing to take on the teaching position, but she wasn't married. He also indicated he would arrange to have a traveling minister hold services at our church once a month as soon as it was finished. With Rev. Wilbur's assurance we would have a teacher ready to start teaching in the fall, we added a small living space on to what we were now calling the community hall.

One day, while Mary and I were working on the building, I watched a young family row their small boat across the river. They approached apprehensively, but when I put forth my hand to shake, they relaxed. They said, "We hear you're building a church that will also be used as a school house. Would it be possible we could worship with you, as well as have our children attend the school?"

Mary smiled, then said, "We'd love to have you do both."

The next day, the young man returned with six men to help finish the construction.

A few weeks later, the first church service and picnic were held, and families from both sides of the river attended. It seemed like the war was finally over, and for the most part, it was.

A year later, it was suggested a graveyard be established alongside the community hall. There was large support for the proposal, until it came out, some families wanted to rebury soldiers who had fought in the Civil War on the side of the Confederacy. The fallout was, the suggestion was tabled, and a few families from the south side of the river stopped attending church services. Some families eventually returned; others never did. A decade later, cemeteries were established on both sides of the river, with no restrictions of who could be buried within.

> *For many centuries, grave markers have served as the primary physical reminder of a life lived. Grave markers and cemeteries have undergone dramatic changes since the mid-1800s. Four places of interment existed in the United States before the nineteenth century: isolated pioneer graves, family farms, churchyards, and potter's fields (for the indigent).*

I understand that besides the church and the school, there was another addition to the valley that helped bring it closer together?

True. In 1876, George Woodham and A. C. Reid built a grist mill on Cedar Creek. Being built on the south side of the river, it gave those families something to be proud of and provided a service to families on both sides of the river.

CHAPTER 6

∞∞∞

The Lamb of God

"It is a great day! We are gathered here to dedicate this building to the Lord. I pray, as our Lord is a beacon of hope to the world, this church shall be a beacon of hope to this valley and surrounding community. For without hope, there is no salvation; and without salvation, there is no peace; and without peace, there is no love. And that's what I came to speak to you about today: love, God's love!

"But before we begin, let me introduce myself. My given name is Augustus, but most people call me Pastor Lamb. When Reverend Wilbur approached me about adding your community to my preaching circuit, I was reluctant, but we prayed together about it, and I prayed again by myself, and then I waited to hear God's voice. I was on my way to meet Rev. Wilbur to tell him no, when I was reminded of a conversation between Jesus and Peter. Jesus asked Peter, 'Do you love me?' And Peter replied, yes, Lord; to which Jesus replied, 'Then feed my sheep!' So here I am. I'm not Peter, but I do love the Lord, and I want to share his love with you!

"Let us bow our heads and open in prayer.

"Forgive me for a short history lesson, but I believe it's hard to understand the present unless we understand the past.

"In the beginning, God created Adam and Eve, and he placed them in the garden of Eden where they communed with God. But Adam and Eve sinned against God, so God removed them from the garden. But this removal did not mean God no longer loved them.

"Time passed. Adam and Eve had two sons, Abel and Cain, and they grew into men. God instructed them each to bring forth a sacrifice as an offering to God, as a covering for their sins. Cain brought forth a sacrifice from his garden, which God rejected. Abel brought forth a lamb and sacrificed it to God, which God accepted. God did not reject Cain's offering because the items he brought forth were tainted or not fit to eat but because his items lacked blood. God was making it clear, only blood, life-giving blood, was an acceptable sacrifice for man's sin.

"Years later, the world's population has grown beyond a mere family to thousands, tens of thousands, hundreds of thousands of people, most of whom have rejected God. But God has a remnant, a chosen people, the Jews. But at this period of time, they are being held captive in Egypt, and have been for generations, until God, through Moses, leads them out of Egypt to the Promised Land of Israel.

"Just before God removes his chosen people from Egypt, He institutes the Passover. Originally, God instructed each Jewish family to cover their doorpost with the blood of a lamb, so the Spirit of God would pass over their homes. Failure to do so would cost the life of their firstborn son. But after entering the Promised Land, God reinstituted the practice of sacrificing a lamb for forgiveness of sin as a yearly celebration.

"Time passes, and the Jewish people and Israel are now under the control of the Roman Empire. God now sends his only Son, Jesus, into the world as a newborn, to save the world. Jesus's sacrifice as the Lamb of God replaces the yearly need for a blood sacrifice during Passover, not only for the Jewish people's sin but for all mankind's sin.

"Now, through Jesus Christ, everyone, Jew and Gentile, can be saved from his sins.

"My favorite verse in the Bible is John 3:16: 'For God so loved the world, that he gave his only begotten Son, that whosoever believeth in him should not perish, but have everlasting life.' What I love about John 3:16 is its simplicity. It strips away all pretension and give us a clear definition of love, and a clear unimpeded pathway to God's love and our personal salvation.

"God: Creator of all things, large and small, including man.

"So loved the world: even though the mankind he created turned its back on him, he provided a one-time sacrifice for all mankind's sin.

"He gave his only begotten Son: Jesus.

"That whosoever believeth in him: places his personal faith in Jesus.

"Should have everlasting life: eternal life.

"My guess is that most of you have heard the story of Jesus's birth. It is the foundation of our celebration of Christmas, a time each year when we give and receive gifts. But what we need to remember is the gift God gave us, his Son, Jesus Christ. Why did God reject Cain's sacrifice? He rejected it because it lacked blood, the only covering God accepts for sin. The Jews were required each year to make a blood sacrifice for their sins, until God sent his only Son, Jesus, as a one-time sacrifice for all people, Jews and Gentiles alike. Jesus is God's Lamb, and God sacrificed him for our sins, and all God requires is our faith.

"I don't know about you, but I personally believe you're never going to get a better deal! By accepting Jesus as your personal Savior, God not only wipes away all your sins, but he then offers you a personal relationship and eternal life in heaven. I ask you to search your heart. I believe God is calling you right now to accept his offer, if you haven't already done so.

"When I preach this message, I am often asked: what must I say to God? Let me reassure you, it's not the words you say that count but the intent of your words!

"I'm going speak to God, and if it's your desire to accept Jesus Christ as your personal Savior, just repeat what I say. It can be out loud or to yourself; I promise God will hear you either way.

"Dear heavenly Father, God of all creation, I come before you today to confess my sins and ask your forgiveness for them. I claim Jesus Christ your Son to be my Savior. I believe he died on the cross as a sacrifice for my sins, and through Jesus my sins have been forgiven. I now have a heavenly Father, and when I die, my spirit will join him in heaven!

"If you prayed this prayer with me, I would like to welcome you to the family of God! I would appreciate it if you would let me know, so I can continue to pray for you. I also have a Bible for you that has a place where we can write your name and the date you accepted Jesus, the Lamb of God, as your personal Savior!"

More than a dozen people came forward to accept Jesus as their Savior, including one of my own children.

Following the church service there was a picnic, which everyone enjoyed. It was also announced at this time, beginning in the fall, school classes would be offered.

CHAPTER 7

∿∿∿

A Son-in-Law and a Daughter-in-Law

THE THIRD TIME I interviewed Thomas, we talked about the years between the building of the community hall and the burn.

As we sat down again, I asked if he enjoyed recounting his memories. He said, "Frankly, yes and no, there are a few things I'd rather forget, while others I'm very fond of. Either way, they were part of my life, and I guess they have made me who I am."

Let's start with what happens after the community hall is christened.

Well, to make a long story short, our children grew up, got married, and became parents. Whitney and Daniel became parents and grandparents as well.

Rev. Wilbur followed through with his promise to provide a school teacher in the fall and a minister for our community church at least once a month.

In late July, Ruth arrived to begin preparing for teaching in the fall. We kept an eye on her, making sure she had the supplies she would need for teaching, as well as her personal needs. She also became a regular at our dinner table several times a week. As it turned out, Mary and I were not the only ones keeping an eye on her. Our son Sam had taken a liking to her as well, and we soon realized the appeal was mutual. By Christmas, it was very clear to everyone they were in love. The New Year brought an engagement, and the end of the school year brought a marriage.

There must have been something in the water or the air, because the traveling minister Rev. Wilbur had secured for our small community church soon became a frequent caller on our daughter Anna. The courting time took a little bit longer, but the results were the same. Anna and Augustus were married a month after Sam and Ruth. A year later, we had grandchildren!

Daniel and I continued to run the sawmill. We had to replace a few parts now and then, due to wear and tear, but it did its job well, until the railroads began being built, and we could not keep up with their demand. In 1874, I met Henry Villard, and we struck up a relationship that would last for the next twenty-five years. We bought not one but two new sawmills and had as many as a dozen men working for us sometimes.

Using the same creek, we replaced the old mill with a new one at the original site and built a second mill further upstream. For nearly two decades, we had standing orders for every railroad tie we could cut.

> *Henry Villard was an American journalist and financier who became president of the Northern Pacific Railway. As a teenager, he immigrated to the United States without his parents' knowledge. Villard became a war correspondent, first covering the American Civil War and later the Austro-Prussian War. While in Germany, Villard became involved in investments in American railroads, and returned to the U.S. in 1874 to oversee his investments in the Oregon and California Railroad. He visited Oregon that summer and, being impressed with the region's natural resources, began acquiring various transportation interests in the region. During the ensuing decade, he acquired several rail and steamship companies and pursued a rail line from Portland to the Pacific Ocean.*

Tell me about orphan trains.

Starting in the 1850s, railroads began the practice of taking orphan children from the East to farm families in the Midwest. The railroad would publicize the date and time the orphan train would be coming through each community. The engineer would blow his whistle several times, and the children would be paraded out to a viewing platform where families could take a look. The youngest children were usually chosen first. After some paperwork, the chosen children went home with their new families, the rest were loaded back on to the train, and the train would roll on to the next town.

In the mid-1870s and early 1880s, Henry Villard arranged for a few orphan trains to come to the Pacific Northwest, with stops in towns between Portland and Seattle. Advertisements were placed in local stores, and information was distributed through most local churches.

Anna and Augustus, after searching their hearts, decided they would like to adopt one of these children. They had a conversation with Mary and me, and we encouraged them to follow their hearts. When they said they would like to adopt a young child, I suggested they keep their hearts open and let the Lord help with the decision-making.

On the day of the orphan train's arrival, Mary and I accompanied Anna and Augustus to the station. It was cold and wet. The older children were paraded out on to the platform while the younger children were kept inside.

I expected Anna and Augustus to ask for permission to see the younger children, but when Peter, a six-year-old boy with dark curly hair, was introduced, it was like God had taken their breath away. After a short glance at each other and with no discussion, both their hands shot up in unison.

After a signing a few papers, we had a new member of the family!

Is it true Peter not only got a new mother and father but a grandfather who took a great deal of interest in him as well? Can you tell me about the relationship between the two of you?

I took him fishing the day after he arrived.

Did he enjoy it?

Doesn't every young boy like to go fishing?

I believe you and Peter have a favorite story.

Yes, it is from the *Grimms' Fairy Tales*.

Which one?

"Hans in Luck."

Why is it your favorite?

Because it teaches a lesson.

HANS IN LUCK

Hans had served his master for seven years, so he said to him, master, my time is up, now I should be glad to go back home to my mother, give me my wages. The master answered, you have served me faithfully and honestly, as the service was, so shall the reward be. And he gave Hans a piece of gold as big as his head. Hans pulled his handkerchief out of his pocket, wrapped up the lump in it, put it on his shoulder, and set out on the way home.

As he went on, always putting one foot before the other, he saw a horseman trotting quickly and merrily by on a lively horse. Ah, said Hans quite loud, what a fine thing it is to ride. There you sit as on a chair, you stumble over no stones, you save your shoes, and cover the ground, you don't know how.

The rider, who had heard him, stopped and called out, hi, there, Hans, why do you go on foot, then. I must, answered he, for I have this lump to carry home, it is true that it is gold, but I cannot hold my head straight for it, and it hurts my shoulder.

I will tell you what, said the rider, we will exchange, I will give you my horse, and you can give me your lump. With all my heart, said Hans, but I can tell you, you will have to crawl along with it.

The rider got down, took the gold, and helped Hans up, then gave him the bridle tight in his hands and said, if you want to go at a really good pace, you must click your tongue and call out, Jup. Jup.

Hans was heartily delighted as he sat upon the horse and rode away so bold and free. After a little while he thought that it ought to go faster, and he began to click with his tongue and call out, Jup. Jup. The horse put himself into a sharp trot, and before Hans knew where he was, he was thrown off and lying in a ditch which separated the field from the highway. The horse would have gone off too if it had not been stopped by a countryman, who was coming along the road and driving a cow before him.

Hans pulled himself together and stood up on his legs again, but he was vexed, and said to the countryman, it is a poor joke, this riding, especially when one gets hold of a mare like this, that kicks and throws one off, so that one has a chance of breaking one's neck.

Never again will I mount it. Now I like your cow, for one can walk quietly behind her, and have, over and above, one's milk, butter and cheese every day without fail. What would I not give to have such a cow. Well, said the countryman, if it would give you so much plea-sure, I do not mind giving the cow for the horse. Hans agreed with the greatest delight, the countryman jumped upon the horse, and rode quickly away.

Hans drove his cow quietly before him, and thought over his lucky bargain. If only I have a morsel of bread—and that can hardly fail me—I can eat butter and cheese with it as often as I like, if I am thirsty, I can milk my cow and drink the milk. My goodness, what more can I want.

When he came to an inn he made a halt, and in his great concern ate up what he had with him—his dinner and supper—and all he had, and with his last few farthings had half a glass of beer. Then he drove his cow onwards along the road to his mother's village.

As it drew nearer mid-day, the heat was more oppressive, and Hans found himself upon a moor which it took about an hour to cross. He felt it very hot and his tongue clave to the roof of his mouth with thirst. I can find a cure for this, thought Hans, I will milk the cow now and refresh myself with the milk. He tied her to a withered tree, and as he had no pail he put his leather cap underneath, but try as he would, not a drop of milk came. And as he set himself to work in a clumsy way, the impatient beast at last gave him such a blow on his head with its hind foot that he fell on the ground, and for a long time could not think where he was.

By good fortune a butcher just then came along the road with a wheelbarrow, in which lay a young pig. What sort of a trick is this cried he, and helped the good Hans up. Hans told him what had happened. The butcher gave him his flask and said, take a drink and refresh yourself. The cow will certainly give no milk, it is an old beast, at the best it is only fit for the plough, or for the butcher. Well, well, said Hans, as he stroked his hair down on his head, who would have thought it. Certainly it is a fine thing when one can kill a beast like that at home, what meat one has. But I do not care much for beef, it is not juicy enough for me. A young pig like that now is the thing to have, it tastes quite different, and then there are the sausages.

Listen, Hans, said the butcher, out of love for you I will exchange, and will let you have the pig for the cow. Heaven repay you for your kindness, said Hans as he gave up the cow, whilst the pig was unbound from the barrow, and the cord by which it was tied was put in his hand.

Hans went on, and thought to himself how everything was going just as he wished, if he did meet with any vexation it was immediately set right. Presently there joined him a lad who was carrying a fine white goose under his arm. They said good morning to each other, and Hans began to tell of his good luck, and how he had always made such good bargains. The boy told him that he was taking the goose to a christening-feast. Just lift her, added he, and laid hold of her by the wings, how heavy she is—she has been fattened up for the last eight weeks. Whosoever has a bite of her when she is roasted will have to wipe the fat from both sides of his mouth. Yes, said Hans, as he weighed her in one hand, she is a good weight, but my pig is no bad one.

Meanwhile the lad looked suspiciously from one side to the other, and shook his head. Look here, he said at length, it may not be all right with your pig. In the village through which I passed, the mayor himself had just had one stolen out of its sty. I fear—I fear that you have got hold of it there. They have sent out some people and it would be a bad business if they caught you with the pig, at the very least, you would be shut up in the dark hole.

The good Hans was terrified. Goodness, he said, help me out of this fix, you know more about this place than I do, take my pig and leave me your goose. I shall risk something at that game, answered the lad, but I will not be the cause of your getting into trouble. So he took the cord in his hand, and drove away the pig quickly along a by-path.

The good Hans, free from care, went homewards with the goose under his arm. When I think over it properly, said he to himself, I have even gained by the exchange. First there is the good roast meat, then the quantity of fat which will drip from it, and which will give me dripping for my bread for a quarter of a year, and lastly the beautiful white feathers. I will have my pillow stuffed with them, and then indeed I shall go to sleep without rocking. How glad my mother will be.

As he was going through the last village, there stood a scissors-grind-er with his barrow, as his wheel whirred he sang, I sharpen scissors and quickly grind, my coat blows out in the wind behind.

Hans stood still and looked at him, at last he spoke to him and said, all's well with you, as you are so merry with your grinding. Yes, answered the scissors-grinder, the trade has a golden foundation. A real grinder is a man who as often as he puts his hand into his pocket finds gold in it. But where did you buy that fine goose?
I did not buy it, but exchanged my pig for it.

And the pig?

That I got for a cow.

And the cow?

I took that instead of a horse.

And the horse?

For that I gave a lump of gold as big as my head.

And the gold?

Well, that was my wages for seven years, service.

You have known how to look after yourself each time, said the grind-er. If you can only get on so far as to hear the money jingle in your pocket whenever you stand up, you will have made your fortune.

How shall I manage that, said Hans. You must be a grinder, as I am, nothing particular is wanted for it but a grindstone, the rest finds itself. I have one here, it is certainly a little worn, but you need not give me anything for it but your goose, will you do it?

How can you ask, answered Hans. I shall be the luckiest fellow on earth. If I have money whenever I put my hand in my pocket, why should I ever worry again? And he handed him the goose and received the grindstone in exchange. Now, said the grinder, as he took up an ordinary heavy stone that lay by him, here is a strong stone for you into the bargain, you can hammer well upon it, and straighten your old nails. Take it with you and keep it carefully. Hans loaded himself with the stones, and went on with a contented heart, his eyes shining with joy. I must have been born with a caul [a special covering], he cried, everything I want happens to me just as if I were a Sunday-child [blest].

Meanwhile, as he had been on his legs since daybreak, he began to feel tired. Hunger also tormented him, for in his joy at the bargain by which he got the cow he had eaten up all his store of food at once. At last he could only go on with great trouble, and was forced to stop every minute, the stones, too, weighed him down dreadfully.

Then he could not help thinking how nice it would be if he had not to carry them just then.

He crept like a snail to a well in a field, and there he thought that he would rest and refresh himself with a cool draught of water, but in order that he might not injure the stones in sitting down, he laid them carefully by his side on the edge of the well. Then he sat down on it, and was to stoop and drink, when he made a slip, pushed against the stones, and both of them fell into the water. When Hans saw them with his own eyes sinking to the bottom, he jumped for joy, and then knelt down, and with tears in his eyes thanked God for having shown him this having any need to reproach himself, from those heavy stones which had been the only things that troubled him.

There is no man under the sun as fortunate as I, he cried out. With a light heart and free from every burden he now ran on until he was with his mother at home.

Why do you like this story so much?

Because it teaches us so many lessons.

What would those be?

First, be satisfied with what you have, not always looking for the next best thing. Second, don't be impulsive. Third, the greater the possessions you have, the greater your troubles and burden will be. Fourth, be aware of those who want to take advantage of you. Lastly, always love your mother, and there's no place like home!

Did you give a special letter to Peter?

I did.

I gave him a letter, and read it to him, and told him he should keep it and read it himself when he learned how to read.

Are you willing to say what it was about?

I can do better than that. I will let you read a copy I made for Mary. The letter explains why *Peter* is an important name and why he should be proud of it.

LETTER TO PETER

> Dear Peter,
>
> I am so proud to have you as my grandson. You are a fine boy and a great fishing partner. Both Grandma and Grandpa want you to know how much we love you, and we are so excited to welcome you to our family.
>
> If you didn't know, Peter is a very important biblical name, so I thought you should know a little about your namesake.
>
> First of all, your name Peter means "rock" or "stone." Keep this in mind, because it is very important!
>
> Now Peter and his brother had been fishing all night in the Sea of Galilee and had caught nothing. (We know what that's like, don't we.) They were cleaning their nets, when Jesus and a large crowd of people who were following Jesus showed up. As the crowd continued grow, Jesus asked Peter if he could borrow his boat, so he might row out a short distance from shore and speak to the people.
>
> After he finished speaking, Jesus said to Peter: "Put out into the deep, and let down your nets for a catch."
>
> And Peter answered, "Master, we have toiled all the night and caught nothing!"
>
> Peter, who had years of experience fishing, was faced with a dilemma: what to do with this instruction from Jesus?
>
> He, his brother, and father had fished all night and caught nothing. He was dead tired after a night of fruitless work. On the other hand, he admired Jesus. He had previously heard Jesus speak, and he had been a witness to the miraculous healing of his mother-in-law and of others who were sick.
>
> Peter answered, "Master, we have toiled all night and caught nothing; nevertheless at your word, I will let down my net."
>
> And when he did, he caught so many fish, his net began to break. He needed two boats to hold them all. Peter was so overcome,

he fell down at Jesus's knees, saying, "Depart from me, for I am a sinful man, O Lord!"

And Jesus said to Peter, "Do not be afraid. From now on, you will catch men." From that day forward, Peter was a disciple for Jesus.

The Bible tells us a great deal about Peter, and while he made many mistakes, he learned from them, and he never lost his love for Jesus.

Although Peter was a Jew, God gave him the task of sharing the good news of God's love with the Gentiles (that's us)!

Remember I told you to remember your name means rock or stone?

In Matthew 16:18, Jesus says, "And so I tell you, Peter, you are a rock, and on this rock foundation I will build my church, and not even death will ever be able to overcome it."

So be proud of your name, but more importantly remember Jesus loves you, and God loves you, and so do Grandpa and Grandma!

How did Peter react to the letter?

He showed it to his parents, and I think they all cried. Anna put the letter away for him to keep it safe and for future reading!

That is great! Next question: what did you do for entertainment?

Once the community hall was finished, it became the center of many social events as well church events. There was usually a square dance once a month, and during the summer months, there were usually a few sporting events, mostly baseball games. I remember once there was a gentleman who came through on his way north from Portland who did a little bit of singing, played the banjo, and told stories and jokes. He was also a ventriloquist and interacted with the audience by telling riddles and seeing if the audience could solve them.

Do you remember an example?

I do. "Many people, by puffing out a breath with too much haste, lose their sight and soon afterwards all consciousness."

What's the answer?

It's a riddle about blowing out a candle before going to bed!

Between 1875 and 1889, before the Washington Territory became a state, what happened within the valley?

Between 1875 and 1889, both sides of the river increased in population. A second community was established about a mile northeast of the original community by A. W. Scott. After several successive years of flooding at the mouth of the Columbia River, the community would become known as Woodland, after its one and only store.

I know we have previously talked about flooding being a seasonal occurrence, and it's why the community at the confluence of the Lewis River and the Columbia River eventually was relocated. But I understand the floods that took place in 1890 and 1894 were more than a seasonal occurrence but real disasters?

It's true the springs of 1890 and 1894 were destructive. It was a combination of heavy snows during the winter and early springs with summer like temperatures. Across both the states of Washington and Oregon, there was significant damage. Personally, in 1890, we lost one of our waterwheels, and the second wheel incurred significant damage. In 1894, we lost both waterwheels, and the second sawmill had to be rebuilt.

> *Disastrous flooding hit the Willamette Valley in 1890 and again in 1894. In Portland, "surging high water covered 250 square blocks and knocked out public utilities . . . . Two drawbridges were stuck open, limiting travel between the east and west sections of the city. Businesses sold merchandise from their second-floor windows or operated from boats floating on city streets." The river reached a high-water mark of 33.5 feet during the inundation, and the flood waters didn't fully recede for three weeks.* [1]

One interesting fact about the 1890 flood was, when the Lewis River receded back within its banks, the flooding had left in front of our place a fairly good-sized island of sand and rock. Ironically, this is where my family and the other valley members took refuge as the Yacolt fire passed by.

Is it true that you have a problem with fish? I thought you liked going fishing!

Not all fish, just some fish.

---

1. Willingham, "Willamette River Flood."

What does that mean?

Well, sometimes, spawning fish choose the stream on which we have our waterwheels. The waterwheels turn the sawmill blades, and if the fish get caught in the wheel, it makes a mess.

Also, during the spring and fall, when the largest runs are taking place, it can be dangerous. The fish migrate to the area where they were born, lay their eggs, and then die. This leaves huge numbers of fish carcasses washed up along the river banks, which attracts predators, mostly bears, but sometimes cougars, which can lead to confrontation. It is always best to carry a gun during these periods of the year.

Do you consume a great deal of fish in your diet?

I would say yes. We catch a large number of fish during the spring and fall and either eat them fresh or smoke them to preserve the meat for later.

I heard there is one type of fish you don't care for.

True, smelt!

What are smelt?

Smelt are a small fish about the size of a small trout, but they are not a freshwater fish. Like salmon and steelhead, they are hatched, then they migrate to the ocean, and eventually, they return to the rivers to spawn again. Unlike salmon, steelhead, and harvest trout, you don't catch smelt with a line and hook but with a net. When they are running, parts of the river look black, and with a dip net you can catch dozens at a time. They usually are six to seven inches long. The best way to prepare them is to smoke them. Some people truly love them but not me! For me, they are best used as bait for much larger fish!

I hear you have a fish story, "Darn Fish," that locals like to tease you about?

I wouldn't, if my wife hadn't told others!

So tell me, and I'll set the record straight.

It was springtime, and the spring Chinook salmon were running. It had been raining every day for two weeks, and all the creeks were overflowing their banks. My wife and I were taking an evening stroll up through the meadow. Our path was dry, but the meadow was covered in six inches of water. As we were strolling along, I looked down and there was this huge salmon trying to swim up the meadow. I jumped off our path and into the field. The water was just above my ankles. I ran to where the fish was floundering around and tried to pick it up, but it squirmed through my arms and back into the flooded field. I ran ahead, and this time I dove on top of it, but it wrangled itself loose again. Hence, the first outburst, "Darn fish!"

Not to be outmuscled by a fish, I got to my feet, and tackled the slippery cuss again, only to come up empty-handed. Which led to the second loud outburst, "Darn fish!"

I looked at my wife, who was laughing, which led to the third loud outburst, "Darn fish!"

The darn fish was now close to making its way back into the creek bed, but I was determined to catch it!

What happened?

I ran over to it, scooped it up in my arms, and was holding it as tight as I could, when with one last flip of its tail, it squirted out from my arms, I fell flat on my face, and the fish landed back in the stream and was gone in an instant. Which led to the last and loudest "darn fish!"

If that had been the end of it, I could have put the incident behind me and moved on, but my lovely wife had to spread the story around. For weeks, I had to hear about it at church, and years later, it still was circulating through the local community.

It's my understanding that several, famous guests have visited your home on their travels. If I give you some names, can you give me your thoughts about these visitors?

I will try. Do I have to be honest?

Let's start with Isaac Stevens.

You mean Napoleon, that's what most of the settlers called him. A reference to his short stature (five feet, four inches) and his penchant for solving his problems with military force rather than with common sense and political negotiations. Isaac was a good man, had a good heart, but was extremely tough (he put judges in jail, if they opposed him), and I would say he was unfair in his dealings with the Indians. He was pro-slavery, yet fought and died defending the Union. I believe, he believed his duty was to make the Washington Territory safe for present and future white settlers at the expense of the Indians. His treatment of Chief Leschi and Chief Kamiakin I didn't agree with. I think future historians will probably be much harsher on him than they are today, but I might be wrong!

What are your thoughts about George McClellan?

My only thoughts about McClellan are he was bright, had a good mind, but was lazy and cut corners. But he could talk and drink, and if you gave him a chance, he would. I always said he was more politician than soldier. Stevens disliked him, called him a liar. He was given the job of exploring the many passes through the Cascade Mountains, to determine the best route for a transcontinental railroad, but instead, he spent the summer fishing. When confronted by Isaac Stevens about his findings, he lied and said there were no passes through the Cascades suitable for a railroad.

What did you think of the author Theodore Winthrop, who wrote "The Canoe and the Saddle," a narrative of his travels through the Washington Territory?

Teddy could talk and was a great storyteller. He stayed with us a couple of times, and we'd visit deep into the night. I remember him telling me a story about a time when he had hired a group of men to porter him and his belongings down a river. He was in a hurry, and he told the men if they increased their pace, he would give them a bonus. Soon, they picked up their pace, but later, he noticed the pace had slowed down and the men were passing a flask of rum around. He grabbed the flask and was threating to toss it into the river if they didn't pick up the pace again. The men threatened to take him ashore and leave him there. So he pulled out his Colt pistol, threw the flask into the river, and ordered his paddlers to return to their task. For the rest of the trip, he kept his gun drawn. When they reached his destination he replaced the flask full of rum and paid them a bonus.

Tell me about Doctor Maynard.

Doctor Maynard was a dear friend. He wanted to go west, but his wife refused to leave the East Coast. So he left her there, and came west on his own. On his way west, he fell in love with a young woman in his wagon train. When he reached Oregon, he petitioned the Court for a divorce, which they granted him. He then married the lovely Catherine Broshears.

Doc had agreed before he left the East Coast that if the community of Olympia would pay for his trip west, he would set up his practice there and remain there for at least one year. After the year was up, he and Catherine came to visit us. He asked my opinion if he should stay in Olympia or head north to a new community just being established called Seattle. I told him I thought he should stay in Olympia, but he didn't listen to me and the rest is history.

Tell me about James Longmire.

James and I were good friends. We met on one of my trips to Olympia way back when. I don't think he ever stayed at our place, but we did visit together many times. Before James, the Oregon Trail began in Missouri and ended at Oregon City. Those who wanted to settle north of the river usually crossed near Fort Vancouver and then followed the Cowlitz River north to Olympia and the Puget Sound. But James Longmire changed that. In 1853, James blazed a new trail across the Cascade Mountain Range—a trail that would have dire consequences for the Indians living in this new path. James is not responsible for the action of others, but he did prove there were passes that could be navigated through the Cascades. Something George McClellan failed to do.

During this period, is there anything that happened you regret or that readers should know about?

I don't know about regret, but your readers should know about the three movements that had a huge impact on the Pacific Northwest during this period of time.

Just to let you know, I might be somewhat tainted in my opinion here, due to the fact that during this period of time, I was making the vast majority of my income from the railroad companies. I will state for the record, I have always tried to treat my employees with respect and paid them a fair wage.

The three movements were populism, progressivism, and unionism. It seemed every new cause at this time ended in "ism." Populism encompassed many things, but at its roots, it was a cause of David versus Goliath. The farmers and small business owners were concerned about the growing trend of economic power being consolidated in the hands of a few powerful and wealthy people—namely, the railroads, banks, and farm equipment manufacturers. The movement wanted the government to provide stability by passing new laws and regulations. The Grange Movement began during this time and moved from being a social institution to a very powerful political organization.

Were you a member of the Grange?

I was, my family was; but for us personally, we enjoyed our membership more as a social institution than as a political organization. But I will say the Grange was a uniting force for small communities that felt they had little or no political power.

Progressivism focused on making government more responsive to the people's wishes. Probably the biggest impact it had on our state was the passage of the initiative and referendum laws. The initiative law gave citizens a pathway to pass laws bypassing the state legislature. It required sponsors to collect a specified number of registered voters' signatures to place a proposed law on the ballot and then let the voters decide if it should become a law. The referendum allowed the state legislature to refer proposed laws directly to the people for a vote. I call this the Coward's Law. It allows elected officials who are afraid they won't get reelected if they vote for a controversial bill to let the proposed law go directly to the people for approval or denial.

What about unionism?

All I have to say about unionism is, some employers take advantage of their employees. They worked them six days a week, ten to twelve hours a day, and often paid them a pittance, which is wrong! My employees work five days a week, unless there is a very important reason, and if we work on Saturday, I pay them extra for their time. We never work on Sunday!

Is it true, your wife was a good friend of Abigail Scott Duniway?

She still is!

Abigail is an amazing woman, almost as amazing as my wife. She championed a cause that was long overdue and refused to give up until she'd won!

God created woman as a helpmate, not a slave. God created women as equals, not inferior to men. Without women, men would accomplish very little other than start wars.

Abigail led the movement for the right of women to vote in Oregon and Washington. She never gave up, and she prevailed! All women in the Pacific Northwest owe her a debt of gratitude.

> Washington nearly became the first state to give women the right to vote in 1854 but failed by one vote.

Lastly, people tell me you have a favorite song you liked to sing at the end of church?

I do.

How does it go?

> All the way my Savior leads me—
> What have I to ask beside?
> Can I doubt His tender mercy,
> Who through life has been my guide?
> Heav'nly peace, divinest comfort,
> Here by faith in Him to dwell!
> For I know, whate'er befall me,
> Jesus doeth all things well;
> For I know, whate'er befall me,
> Jesus doeth all things well.
>
> All the way my Savior leads me—
> Cheers each winding path I tread,
> Gives me grace for ev'ry trial,
> Feeds me with the living bread.
> Though my weary steps may falter
> And my soul athirst may be,
> Gushing from the rock before me,
> Lo! a spring of joy I see;
> Gushing from the rock before me,
> Lo! A spring of joy I see.
>
> All the way my Savior leads me–
> Oh, the fullness of His love!
> Perfect rest to me is promised
> In my Father's house above.
> When my spirit, clothed immortal,
> Wings its flight to realms of day,

This my song through endless ages:
Jesus led me all the way;
This my song through endless ages:
Jesus led me all the way.

This was my grandfather's last interview with Thomas.

What follows is the original story my grandfather wrote about the Yacolt fire, "Hero of the Yacolt Burn."

Oregon Journal [Newspaper]
"Hero of the Yacolt Burn"

By T. Y. Elliot   September 16, 1902

As the fires raging across Northwest Oregon and Southwest Washington continue to smolder, it is clear the devastation is of epic proportion. Estimates put the total number of acreage destroyed at over 200,000 acres and the death toll now stands at 38 known victims. The cause of the fire as of this publication has not been determined. Some sources cite lightning strikes, while others report the fire began as a slash burn that got out of control. Still others are placing the fault on careless campers.

It has been confirmed the fire started near Bridal Veil, Oregon. Strong westerly winds stoked the fire, causing burning debris to carry across the Columbia River to Washington State. The fire is now burning in the counties of Clark, Cowlitz, and Skamania. Although the fire has officially been given the name Yacolt Burn, the small community of Yacolt has been spared. One local citizen reported the inferno blistered the paint on local homes before veering north towards the Lewis River Valley.

Once the fire reached the Lewis River Valley, strong winds began pushing it west towards the Columbia River. I must sadly report the largest loss of human life has taken place in this valley.

Local residents are now hailing Thomas Merriman, his son, and son-in-law as heroes for saving the lives of many locals, while placing their own lives in jeopardy.

I interviewed Mr. Merriman about what happened on that fateful day. "The dog woke me up from barking, so I got up to start the coffee pot. When I looked outside, the sky was burnt red. I stepped outside and all I could see were bellows of smoke, as high as I could see.

"I woke the wife and told her to grab a few items and head for the river. I hitched the wagon and headed for my son and son-in-law's places. I roused them and told them to get their families to the river, and then one was to go north, the other west, to warn neighbors. 'I'm headed east,' I said, 'Everyone should gather on the small island in middle of the river.'

"I then headed east, stopping at each home and giving the same instructions. The further east I traveled, the worse it got. Once I reached the crest of the hill, I could see the fire. The flames were jumping from tree to tree and headed straight down the valley. When I arrived at the last house it was possible to reach, they were packing their wagon. I told them there was no time, just get in their wagon and go. I then headed towards my place and the river. When I reached the river, there were probably a hundred souls there, and within a few minutes, another twenty or more souls arrived.

"Within the hour, the fire swept right past us! Everyone we had gathered survived. The next day, we found those we hadn't reached."

CHAPTER 8

So Many Changes

BETWEEN 1880 AND 1910, there were so many changes.

The vast majority of train track had been laid across the West.

> *In 1881, the Northern Pacific Railroad reached Spokane. In 1893, the Great Northern Railway reached Seattle.*
>
> *A negative impact of the Continental Railroad was the near demise of the bison (called **buffalo** in that time period). In 1893, the U.S. government reported there were only two thousand bison left roaming the plains, where once millions roamed.*

The need for large amounts of railroad ties was slowing down, and so were Thomas's sawmill orders. For the first time in years, he had to lay off employees. Not only were the times changing, so were improvements in technology.

The donkey engine transformed logging in the Pacific Northwest. Equipment began replacing manpower. Small mills like Thomas's would soon be replaced by mega-mills that ran twenty-four hours a day, with hundreds of employees each.

> *In 1881, John Dolbeer invented the donkey engine and revolutionized*

logging. The donkey engine was a single-cylinder steam engine connected to a large spindle. By wrapping cables around the spindle, the engine pulled huge loads that would otherwise require animal power. The skid road and the ox team were rendered obsolete. The first donkey engine in the Pacific Northwest appeared at the Blanchard Lumber Company's operation on Bellingham Bay in 1887.

In 1889, Washington became the forty-second state in the Union.

A year later, the population of Seattle reached 42,837. Tacoma's population was reported as 36,006; but Portland was still the largest city in the Pacific Northwest, with a population of 46,385. That changed in 1897, when the discovery of gold in the Klondike started a new gold rush, which had a huge impact on the Washington Territory, especially the city of Seattle.

When it came to lumber, the biggest change was not what but who. Frederick Weyerhäuser and R. A. Long began moving their logging and mill operations into the Pacific Northwest.

In 1900, Frederick Weyerhäuser bought 900,000 acres of timberland in the Pacific Northwest from James Hill and founded the Weyerhaeuser Timber Company. He immediately became the largest producer of lumber in the Northwest. The Weyerhaeuser Company is still the world's largest producer of lumber products.

As times changed, Thomas kept in step. He decided to open two lumber yards, one in Vancouver, Washington, and another in Portland, Oregon. The idea was to make it easier for people to buy the lumber they needed when they needed it, without waiting or having to travel to a mill. He also began the process of selling lumber to builders of homes at a discounted price. Soon, he was making as much money from his lumber yards as he was from his sawmill and was able to rehire some of the employees he had previously laid off. Within a few years, he doubled his lumber yards, adding one in the community located at the mouth of the Cowlitz River and one further north in Olympia.

The addition of the lumber yards allowed both Thomas and Mary to relax a little. With the fear of financial ruin behind them, they set about to enjoy life again. The house once again became the host for a long list of friends and dignitaries. They took trips to San Francisco and Vancouver Island. The last trip Thomas and Mary made together was in the summer of 1910. They took the train to Seattle to visit the Alaska-Yukon-Pacific Exposition. According to Peter, their grandson who accompanied them, they reminisced about their days of crossing the Oregon Trail, the building of the first sawmill together, the birth of Sam and Anna, and how much things had changed in their lifetime!

CHAPTER 9

Funeral for a Friend

On July 1, 1912, I received a telegram from Augustus: Thomas had passed away in his sleep on June 30th. The family was planning a small funeral ceremony, but as word of Thomas's death began to circulate, friends and acquaintances were wanting something larger as a tribute to this amazing man. Businessmen, politicians, and friends from near and far wanted to say their last goodbyes.

Augustus asked if I would be willing to say a few words, since I was the one who made him famous nationwide. I said, the truth is, I did very little to increase Thomas's notoriety. He did that himself through honest interaction with everyone he ever met; but I would be honored to say a few words in celebration of his life.

It was a beautiful July afternoon. I arrived early to see if I could help with anything. Augustus and Peter were greeting guests. I said it's a beautiful day; Thomas would have wanted it this way. In my mind, I could see him sitting on the riverbank fishing!

I recognized former Governor Henry McBride and current Governor Marron Hay. There were representatives from the Northern Pacific Railroad and the Great Northern Railway. I said my greetings to Abigail Scott Duniway and to the daughter of Mrs. McCleary and gave my condolences to Ann, as I made my way over to embrace Mary.

The ceremony began with a welcome from Augustus and a small tribute to his father-in-law.

He said, "The first time I met Thomas, I was with Rev. Wilbur. I didn't say too much, but I listened intently to their plans for this small community church. I was a traveling pastor at the time, and my first thought was, I already have too many other Churches I'm serving, to meet the needs of this community church as well.

"But God and Thomas changed my mind, and I am so glad they did, because if they hadn't, I would not be here today! I wouldn't have known the generosity and kindness of the man who would eventually become my father-in-law, and a true friend.

"I've been told the story of how Thomas shared with his wife Mary the importance of her name, and he did the same with my son Peter. Today, I'd like to share with you about the name Thomas!

"We often associate the name Thomas with the biblical story of doubting Thomas. The Bible states, Thomas was not with the other disciples when Jesus appeared to them the first time, and when the disciples shared the news they had seen Jesus, he did not believe them. It's recorded Thomas said, 'I will not believe until I can touch his wounds.'

"When Jesus appeared to the disciples a second time, Thomas was there, and Jesus invited Thomas to touch his wounds, but instead Thomas showed his belief by saying 'My Lord and my God.' Jesus then said to Thomas, 'Because you have seen me, you have believed: blessed are they that have not seen, and yet have believed.' Thomas Merriman was one of the very blessed: he lived a life full of faith!

"On one of my first visits, I asked Thomas how and when he accepted Jesus as his Savior, and this is what he shared with me:

"'My father owned a sawmill, and sometimes I rode along with him on his delivery trips to Independence and we'd talk. He'd tell me stories from the Bible, and I'd listen intently. He always said, there are five important things to having a good life. If you always work hard and are honest, people will respect you; the closest thing to heaven you will experience here on earth is the love of your family, so love your wife like she's the most precious thing on this earth and raise your children to be God-fearing, and they will be a joy and not a burden. Be resolute and never be afraid to dream; but, above all, love God with all your heart.

"'I remember asking him, how do you love God with all your heart?

"'He said, "First, you have to ask God into your heart, and you do that by placing your faith in God's Son, Jesus. The Bible says in John 3:16, 'For God so loved the world, that He gave His only begotten Son, that whosoever believeth in Him should not perish, but have everlasting life.'"'

"'So, I bowed my head and repeated John 3:16 and asked Jesus into my heart.'

"I know as sure as I am standing here, we are going to bury Thomas's body today in our local graveyard, but his soul is in heaven with the Lord!

"The family has asked several friends of Thomas's to share with you."

As I looked around, there wasn't a dry eye, and that included me!

I did not grow up in a Christian home, and maybe my job as a newspaper reporter had made me more cynical, but I realize the truth when I hear it. So, I closed my eyes, repeated John 3:16 to myself, and asked Jesus into my heart.

The tears were once again falling from my eyes, but this time they were tears of joy! I felt like a huge weight had been lifted off my soul, a weight I hadn't even realized existed. I wanted to tell everyone, but I realized this was not the time or place, so I silently shared it only with Thomas!

I was the last scheduled speaker. All of the others had given such moving tributes, I prayed I could be as respectful to a true legend.

I looked out at the faces and smiled, because Thomas would have wanted it that way.

"I believe most of you are aware I penned the tribute 'Hero of the Yacolt Burn' about Thomas, but what you might not know is, in the aftermath of the fire, we became very good friends. I interviewed him several times about his life, and he gave me the journal he kept about his experiences on the Oregon Trail to read, which I did, and then faithfully returned to him.

"Thomas's life reads like a fairy tale in many ways, but in other ways, it was filled with heartache and pain. The good news is, there was much greater joy than sadness!

"I have chosen a few of his life's experiences to share with you. Thomas, I know you're listening!

"The first thing I'd like to share about Thomas is, he was not the first pioneer in his family. His parents packed up their lives and moved from West Virginia to Missouri in 1828. Thomas was five at the time.

"Like many fathers, Thomas's father worked long hours to provide for his family, leaving little time for a young boy who desperately desired his father's attention. The precious little time he had with his father was extra special. The things Thomas looked forward to the most were bedtime stories and rides with his father when he delivered lumber. He told me, when his father started telling a story, he'd close his eyes, and he could see the characters come to life!

"The first traumatic experience Thomas faced was the loss of his father, which would soon be compounded by the marriage of his mother to another man.

"Thomas expressed to me, it took years for him to sort out his real feelings and understand the real reason he left Missouri to come to Oregon was because he felt abandoned and unloved.

"I'm not sure if Thomas had a very vivid imagination or a gift of seeing the future through his dreams, but he recorded in his journal several dreams he had during his travel across the Oregon Trail. I asked him if he thought these were premonitions, to which he replied, 'They were probably just caused by indigestion!'

"But his dreams had a canny way of often coming true, especially when they were about Mary!

"After leaving Missouri, the two most important people in his life became Mary and her then-husband Sam. Thomas eventually asked if they wanted to form a partnership in a sawmill business with him, to which they agreed.

"To say the least, Thomas was a little naïve. Once, a young woman who was seeking a husband asked Thomas to join her on a picnic. Thomas didn't know (and neither did I), on the Oregon Trail, *picnic* was the code word for sneaking away for marital relations. If it hadn't been for Mary who had overheard the conversation and intervened, Thomas would have been married at the next fort, whether he liked it or not!

"There was also the time when Sam told him Mary had morning sickness. Thomas had no clue what that meant! And my favorite is his story about bathing naked in a stream with another wagon train member, oblivious to fact she was a woman!

"Like many who traveled across the Oregon Trail, Thomas wanted to leave his mark, I mean literally, so he carved his name on the limestone bluff known as Register Cliff.

"He was a huge fan of baseball or, as he called it, 'rounders' and a pretty good fiddle player, if he said so himself!

"There aren't too many of us, if any, that can say they once lived in a pit house. But Thomas could!

"Thomas was one of the first settlers to plant apple trees in what would become the state of Washington. I ate a few of them, and they were nice and juicy.

> *Washington State grows 175,000 acres of apples. That is almost 60% of the U.S. supply and the most valuable crop in Washington State.*

"In one of the first years he lived in the Oregon Territory, the Columbia River actual froze, and local residents put ice skates on and skated across the river and back. Thomas tried several times to skate but after many falls, he decided he'd rather stand by the fire and watch others make fools of themselves. His ego was plenty big enough to handle the small amount of ribbing he endured while watching those who could skate!

"Morning surprise! He went to bed one night, and when he woke up the next morning, his field was full of teepees. His first response was, where did they all come from? His next response was, I always wondered why there was this large open field here with no trees; now I know!

"He told me the hardest thing he ever endured was the death of Sam and the subsequent heartache Mary felt. But the greatest joy he ever felt was when Mary agreed to marry him.

"My memories of the holidays have always been special, he said—not because of the gifts, of which most were clothes, but more because of the traditions. Before his father passed away, they always gathered as an extended family and would take turns reading from the Bible about the birth of Jesus—even if it was just one sentence, with help from their mother. So, when he suggested to Mary they read from the family Bible his mother had given to him, and she said no, he was hurt. He wasn't sure how to react until she started crying and said, I don't know how to read. So, he taught Mary how to read.

"The truth is he taught so many of us something: about how to be a good neighbor, about being tolerant towards others, how to be a responsible employer, how to be a friend, how to love.

How to say goodbye: goodbye, my friend!

The family has one last request. Will you please stand and sing Thomas's favorite song?

All the way my Savior leads me—
What have I to ask beside?
Can I doubt His tender mercy,
Who through life has been my guide?
Heav'nly peace, divinest comfort,
Here by faith in Him to dwell!
For I know, whate'er befall me,
Jesus doeth all things well;
For I know, whate'er befall me,
Jesus doeth all things well.

All the way my Savior leads me—
Cheers each winding path I tread,
Gives me grace for ev'ry trial,
Feeds me with the living bread.
Though my weary steps may falter
And my soul athirst may be,
Gushing from the rock before me,
Lo! a spring of joy I see;
Gushing from the rock before me,
Lo! A spring of joy I see.

All the way my Savior leads me—
Oh, the fullness of His love!
Perfect rest to me is promised
In my Father's house above.
When my spirit, clothed immortal,
Wings its flight to realms of day,
This my song through endless ages:
Jesus led me all the way;
This my song through endless ages:
Jesus led me all the way.

CHAPTER 10

‹‹‹

The Final Pages of This Story

IT TOOK TIME, BUT I finally finished my additions to my great-grandfather's manuscript. I sent it to the print shop, and I ordered a dozen copies. I figured I'd hand out a few to family members and send off a few to book publishers.

But it was the last two for which I had special plans!

When I got my copies, I took two copies and put them aside. I then went to my kitchen, took out the two tins I had purchased for this special occasion, and placed inside each of the tins a copy of Great-Grandfather's manuscript. I then sealed each tin with tape. I wrote on the outside of the first tin "To Great-Grandpa, from your Great-Grandson" and on the second tin "To Thomas: even though we never met, it seems like I know you like a best friend."

A few days later, on Saturday, I woke up early, got dressed, carefully picked up the two tins and got in my car. I had a plan, but I hadn't realized until I began executing it how much I had become emotionally attached to this project. My first stop was at the cemetery where my great-grandfather is buried. I took our manuscript, safe from the elements in a sealed tin, and laid it against his headstone at his grave. I took a few minutes and told him all about the journey his story about the "Hero of the Yacolt Burn" had taken. And how much I had enjoyed retracing the journey with him.

I then resumed my travel, which led me to the Lewis River Valley and the small cemetery were Thomas Merriman is buried. I found his gravestone, just a plain stone, with his name and dates of birth and death. But unlike my great-grandfather, he was surrounded by family. Mary was next to him, and nearby were Ann and Sam, as were Daniel and Whitney. I felt like I knew them all so well. I left the second tin next to Thomas's headstone, said my goodbyes, and drove back home. It was an emotional day!

A few weeks later, I was at work when the phone rang. I picked it up with my usual phrase, "This is Tyler Elliot, how can I help you?"

At first there was only silence, then a voice said, "My name is Peter, and my father was the grandson of Thomas Merriman!"

THE END

Referenced Works

"1803 Louisiana Purchase." Compromise of 1850, n.d. http://www.com-promise-of-1850.org/1803-louisiana-purchase/.

Alchin, Linda. "Flathead Native Indians." War Paths 2 Peace Pipes, Nov. 20, 2012; updated Jan. 16, 2018. https://www.warpaths2peacepipes.com/indian-tribes/flatheads.htm.

Animals Network Team. "Jackrabbit." Animals, twainquotes.com/Rabbit.html.

"Animism." Wikipedia, last edited Apr. 10, 2022. https://en.wikipedia.org/wiki/Animism.

"Blue Mountains (Pacific Northwest)." Wikipedia, last edited Dec. 24, 2021. https://en.wikipedia.org/wiki/Blue_Mountains_(Pacific_Northwest).

Brooke, Bob. "On the Oregon Trail, Hardship Piled on Hardship—Yet Brave Travelers Kept Going." HistoryNet, Mar. 17, 2022. https://www.historynet.com/what-was-it-like-on-the-oregon-trail/.

Brown, David W. "Ten Facts about the Real-Life Oregon Trail." Mental Floss, Mar. 1, 2016. https://www.mentalfloss.com/article/69250/10-fun-facts-about-real-life-oregon-trail.

"Cedar Creek Grist Mill." Cedar Creek Grist Mill, n.d. https://www.cedarcreekgristmill.org.

"Cholera." Wikipedia, last edited May 11, 2022. https://en.wikipedia.org/wiki/Cholera.

Crosby, Fanny. "All the Way My Savior Leads Me." Hymnary, 1875. https://hymnary.org/text/all_the_way_my_savior_leads_me.

"Cyrus the Great." Wikipedia, last edited May 11, 2022. https://en.wikipedia.org/wiki/Cyrus_the_Great.

Editors, History.com. "Santa Fe Trail." History, Jan. 17, 2018; updated June 3, 2019. https://www.history.com/topics/westward-expansion/santa-fe-trail.

Erie, Grace. "Ten Things You Probably Didn't Know about the Oregon Trail." Little Things, Feb. 6, 2017. https://littlethings.com/lifestyle/life-on-the-oregon-trail.

Fixico, Donald, interview. "The Transcontinental Railroad; Interview: Native Americans." American Experience, n.d. https://www.pbs.org/wgbh/americanexperience/features/tcrr-interview/.

"Fort Hall." Wikipedia, last edited Feb. 1, 2022. https://en.wikipedia.org/wiki/Fort_Hall.

"Fort Kearny." Wikipedia, last edited Mar. 22, 2022. https://en.wikipedia.org/wiki/Fort_Kearny.

"Fort Vancouver." Wikipedia, Feb. 20, 2022. https://en.wikipedia.org/wiki/Fort_Vancouver.

"Frederick Weyerhäuser." Wikipedia, last edited Jan. 16, 2022. https://en.wikipedia.org/wiki/Friedrich_Weyerhäuser.

"George Bush (Pioneer)." Wikipedia, last edited May 15, 2022. https://en.wikipedia.org/wiki/George_Bush_(pioneer).

"Henry Villard." Wikipedia, last edited July 11, 2021. https://en.wikipedia.org/wiki/Henry_Villard.

"History of Spokane, Washington." Wikipedia, last edited Apr. 21, 2022. https://en.wikipedia.org/wiki/History_of_Spokane,_Washington.

"History of Washington Apples." Washington Apple Commission, n.d. https://waapple.org/did-you-know/.

"Jason Lee (Missionary)." Wikipedia, last edited Feb. 22, 2022. https://en.wikipedia.org/wiki/Jason_Lee_(missionary).

"Lewis River (Washington)." Wikipedia, last edited Nov. 11, 2021. https://en.wikipedia.org/wiki/Lewis_River_(Washington).

"Manifest Destiny." Wikipedia, last edited Apr. 13, 2022. https://en.wikipedia.org/wiki/Manifest_destiny.

"Missouri River." Wikipedia, last edited Apr. 1, 2022. https://en.wikipedia. org/wiki/Missouri_River.

"Monticello Convention." Wikipedia, last edited Dec. 17, 2020. https:// en.wikipedia.org/wiki/Monticello_Convention.

Oldham, Kit. "Bush, George (1780?–1863)." HistoryLink, Jan. 31, 2004. https://historylink.org/file/5645.

"Oregon Trail." Wikipedia, last edited Apr. 11, 2022. https://en.wikipedia. org/wiki/Oregon_Trail.

"Pemmican." Wikipedia, last edited Mar. 18, 2022. https://en.wikipedia. org/wiki/Pemmican.

"Platte River." Wikipedia, last edited Feb. 24, 2022. https://en.wikipedia. org/wiki/Platte_River.

"Puget Sound." Wikipedia, Mar. 30, 2022. https://en.wikipedia.org/wiki/ Puget_Sound.

"Salmon Falls (Snake River)." Wikipedia, last edited Oct. 22, 2020. https:// en.wikipedia.org/wiki/Salmon_Falls_(Snake_River).

Sheller, Roscoe. "Snipes, Ben, Northwest Cattle King: A Talk by Roscoe Sheller." History Link, orig. Apr. 1958; posted Mar. 15, 2005. People's History Collection. https://www.historylink.org/file/7265.

"Soda Springs." History Globe, n.d. Historyglobe.com/ot/sodasprings. htm.

"South Pass (Wyoming)." Wikipedia, last edited Jan. 6, 2022. https:// en.wikipedia.org/wiki/South_Pass_(Wyoming).

"Snake River." Wikipedia, last edited Apr. 5, 2022. https://en.wikipedia. org/wiki/Snake_River.

"Thomas Fitzpatrick (Trapper)." Wikipedia, last edited Jan. 6, 2022. https://en.wikipedia org/wiki/Thomas_Fitzpatrick_(trapper).

"Three Island Crossing." Wikipedia, last edited Jan. 8, 2020. https:// en.wikipedia.org/wiki/Three_Island_Crossing.

Tucker, Kathy. "James H. Wilbur." Oregon Encyclopedia, last updated Mar. 30, 2022. https://www.oregonencyclopedia.org/articles/wilbur_ james_h_1811_1887_/#.YltF9C-B1hA.

"Voting Rights for Women, Women's Suffrage." Washington Secretary of State, n.d. www.sos.wa.gov/elections/timeline/suffrage.htm.

Ward, Jean M. "Abigail Scott Duniway (1834–1915)." Oregon Encylopedia, last updated Mar. 11, 2022. https://www.oregonencyclopedia.org/articles/abigail_scott_duniway/#.Yn8CpujMK5d.

Willingham, William F. "Willamette River Flood of 1894." Oregon Encyclopedia, last updated Mar. 31, 2022. https://www.oregonencyclopedia.org/articles/willamette_flood_1894_/#.YltHwS-B1hA.

Wilma, David. "John Dolbeer Invents the Donkey Engine and Revolutionizes Logging in August 1881." HistoryLink, Mar. 1, 2003. https://historylink.org/File/5331.

Wilma, David. "Yacolt Burn, Largest Forest Fire in Recorded Washington History to That Point, Rages for Three Days Beginning on September 11, 1902." History Link, Feb. 14, 2003; updated July 22, 2014; corrected Apr. 19, 2016. https://historylink.org/File/5196.